*S*pirits
Between the Bays
Series

Delaware Bay

Chesapeake Bay

Volume VIII

*H*orror

in the

*H*allway

Ed Okonowicz

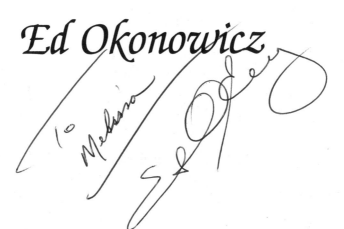

To Melissa
Ed O.

Spirits Between the Bays
Volume VIII
Horror in the Hallway
First Edition

ISBN 1-890690-04-X

Published by
Myst and Lace Publishers, Inc.
1386 Fair Hill Lane
Elkton, Maryland 21921

Printed in the U.S.A.
by Victor Graphics

Cover Art, Typography and Design
by Kathleen Okonowicz

Dedications

In memory of my Aunt Marie Bartol Okonowicz.
For Cousin Marie, my fourth sister.
For Captain Ron, the man's a saint.
Ed Okonowicz

In memory of my Uncle Leo Burgoon.
Kathleen Burgoon Okonowicz

Acknowledgments

The author and illustrator appreciate the assistance of those
who have played an important role in this project.
Special thanks are extended to
Louis and Joyce Andrew, Ruth Citro, Bob Cohen,
Debbie and Loren Leach and
Dave and Judy Pugh for their valuable assistance;
and to

John Brennan
Barbara Burgoon
Sue Moncure
Marianna Dyal
Ted Stegura and
Monica Witkowski
for their proofreading and suggestions;

and, of course,

particular appreciation to the ghosts and their hosts.

Also available from
Myst and Lace Publishers, Inc.

Spirits Between the Bays Series

Volume I
Pulling Back the Curtain
(October, 1994)

Volume II
Opening the Door
(March, 1995)

Volume III
Welcome Inn
(September, 1995)

Volume IV
In the Vestibule
(August, 1996)

Volume V
Presence in the Parlor
(April, 1997)

Volume VI
Crying in the Kitchen
(April, 1998)

Volume VII
Up the Back Stairway
(April, 1999)

Volume VIII
Horror in the Hallway
(September, 1999)

DelMarVa Murder Mystery Series
FIRED!
(May, 1998)

Halloween House
(May, 1999)

Stairway over the Brandywine
A Love Story
(February, 1995)

Possessed Possessions
Haunted Antiques, Furniture and Collectibles
(March, 1996)

Possessed Possessions 2
More Haunted Antiques, Furniture and Collectibles
(September, 1998)

Disappearing Delmarva
Portraits of the Peninsula People
(August, 1997)

Table of Contents

Introduction   1

True Stories

Legend and Lore

 Site is open to the public.

 Story is about a haunted possession.

Introduction

W elcome to *Horror in the Hallway*, Vol. VIII of our 13-
volume *Spirits Between the Bays* ghost/folklore series. As
in our seven earlier volumes, we have included stories
that we hope will make you uneasy and uncomfortable, especially
if you are brave enough to read this book in the late evening,
when you are home alone beside a flickering fire.

A new addition to our Spirits series are stories about haunted
antiques, furniture and collectibles. Previously, we published two
volumes focusing on *Possessed Possessions*, and we continue to
receive reports of unusual events from the owners of more troubled objects from across the country. To share these delightfully
horrifying stories, we will incorporate the best of these new haunted object tales in our Spirits books.

One suggestion: Don't plan to read the stories of the "Deadly
Violin" or the "Bargain Bed?" late in the evening, unless you want
to have a very restless night. They are two of the most troubling
tales about haunted objects that I have found.

This volume contains some stories that were told to me within the last few months, but several others—like "Spirit of Rutledge
House," "Slammin' and Bammin' " and "Pretty in Pink"—have been
waiting for several years to find their way onto the printed page.
As I worked on this volume, I was amazed at how different and
unusual some of these stories are. They all deal with the supernatural, but each has a special twist, a particular identity of its

own. It was a lot of fun putting this collection together. We hope you will find these stories as interesting as we did when we heard them for the first time.

There's one other thing to note about this book. Several of the incidents featured in the chapter entitled "Short Sightings" occurred at sites that have been featured in previous books in our series. In a sense, these new events add credibility to the original stories, and that's always satisfying to discover.

We appreciate your patronage and enjoy meeting many of you at public events and book signings.

Coming up next: HOSTAGE: *DelMarVa Murder Mystery* #3 and Vol. IX, *Phantom In the Bedchamber.*

Happy Hauntings.

—Ed Okonowicz
in Fair Hill, Maryland,
at the northern edge
of the Delmarva Peninsula
—Fall 1999

Spirit of Rutledge House

I can't tell you where this house is—won't even mention the name of the town. All I'll share about its location is that it's a stately structure on a tree-lined street in the oldest section of a well-known, larger-sized, Eastern Shore town. Of course, a residence of this age and stature has a name, and since I can't provide the real name, I should use something fictional but appropriate. Let's call it the Rutledge House. That sounds old and elegant enough. Yes. the Rutledge House it is.

But enough hazy details about the location, now onto the story. Everything else in this chapter—except the names of the current owners—is exactly as it was told to me.

I received directions to Rutledge House. Even though it was situated among more than two dozen other attractive, late 19th-century, Victorian-style residences, Rutledge House stood out among the rest.

It's eyelash windows, second- and third-floor balconies, turrets and stained glass windows made passers-by stop and notice. But the fascinating exterior offered only an inkling of the amazing architectural details and extra added features that rested inside.

U.S. and Maryland flags stood on either side of the steps leading to the wide wrap-around porch. Jake met me at the wood-framed, screened front door. His wife, Ellie, was seated on an antique swing-type glider beneath a slow-turning Casablanca fan on the rear section of the porch.

3

After a quick tour of the three levels, we settled into white wicker furniture and began to talk. In the background you could hear the croaking of frogs and enjoy the twinkling display offered by hundreds of floating fireflies.

The couple bought the home in 1970, nearly 30 years ago. They moved down from southeast Pennsylvania to enjoy the calm countryside and nature.

Jake provided a quick rundown on the building's history.

The house was built by an Eastern Shore merchant and landowner who spared no expense in the construction. The home's six working fireplaces are made of brick shipped from England. Wood paneling and matching overhead beams accent plaster walls throughout the entire home.

Columns of genuine marble, imported from Italy, support the ceiling of a ballroom on the third level. Obviously, entertainment was an important part of the owner/builder's life.

The three-acre plot includes a professionally designed, manicured garden. The house was placed in the center of the wide lot to insure that neighbors would be kept outside of hearing range of the Rutledge House occupants. Jake pointed out that the present landscape design is very similar to that which was placed around the home when it had been built.

But things did not go well for the home's first owner.

"The way I hear the story," Jake said, "and there are still people who don't like to talk about it, the original builder went all out to use only the best materials and builders for his home. Everything is first rate; even in the servants' quarters the quality is as good as the construction on the first floor and ballroom. That's because he built this place for his girlfriend. She was from New York City and a showgirl or dancer in one of the revues up there. I don't know the exact shows she was in, or even her name, but I do know that folks say she was a knockout and was definitely in show business. He built it as a present for her. Then he brought her down and they lived together—unmarried—for about a year and a half."

At this point, Ellie entered the conversation. "You have to keep in mind that this was small town America."

"Still is!" interjected Jake, adding a hearty laugh.

After tossing her husband a pair of rolled eyes, Ellie continued, "As I was saying, at the turn of the century you did not live with someone to whom you were not married. So the owner and his lady friend were the talk of the town."

"But that didn't stop the rest of the bigshots from coming to their parties," Jake said, laughing. "They say this place was always hopping. People coming from Balt'mer, New York, Philly. Apparently, this young lady had a lot of friends on the vaudeville or show circuits, and they would use this house as a stopover or vacation spot. It didn't seem to bother the rich boyfriend. As long as his lady was happy, so was he."

Unfortunately, the merchant/builder's luck did not hold out. Within two years after he had moved into his dream home, authorities discovered that he had stolen funds from his business partners. He was arrested, convicted and promptly shipped off to prison.

"That was the end of the parties and the girlfriend," Jake said. "She packed up and went back to New York and never returned. Soon, another family moved in—the Rutledges—and that's how the house got its name. They lived here from the early 1900s until we came along in 1970. That's a long time for a family to live in one house, and the name stuck. Even today, after almost 30 years, people still call it the Rutledge House. But we don't mind, just as long as we can live here."

"The story goes," Ellie said, almost whispering, "that the girl-friend died in New York, but she liked her house so much that her spirit has come back to live here. And that makes sense, since it was built for her in the first place."

Nodding in agreement, Jake explained that the Rutledges, a prominent business family, enjoyed the home. "Their children always had parties and the parents also did a lot of entertaining," he said. "When they sold the place to us, they said they were happy because we have four children, and they could tell their house was going to a happy family."

Soon after Ellie and Jake moved in, they noticed little things happening that were more annoying than frightening. Personal items would disappear and then reappear; lights would go on and off (but Jake figured the wiring was old and starting to fall apart), certain parts of the house were colder than others, plus there were occasional sounds associated with shutting doors and unex-plained footsteps.

"No one could put a finger on anything definite," Jake said, "but there was this feeling in the air—coupled with all the strange things I just mentioned—that someone or something was around."

One morning, Ellie was in the kitchen cooking while her youngest daughter was playing nearby with a small plastic plate. The child rolled the disc down the small hallway—off the kitchen near the stairway to the old servants' quarters—and the plate disappeared.

"It was gone," Ellie said. "It couldn't have gone anywhere. The back of that hall is a dead end, and the plate was gone. It dematerialized. I called Jake in from outside to tell him what happened. We both looked for it, but it was gone."

On a particularly uneasy evening, Jake said neither he nor Ellie nor any of the children could sleep. It was a restless night, like there was strange unbridled energy moving from room to room. One of the daughters ran into her parents' room during early morning darkness and said she saw people flying in the air over her bed.

Very early the next morning, a neighbor called to tell Ellie and Jake that Mrs. Rutledge, from whom Jake and Ellie had bought the home, had died suddenly in the middle of the night.

"Even before that, we had begun to put two and two together," Jake said, "but after that night we knew for sure something strange was going on in here. Now, over the next several years, on three or four different occasions—from people that don't know each other and who we have never told anything—we have heard that there is definitely a spirit in our house. And what makes it more believable, is that they all have described the woman in a similar way."

I noticed that Jake consistently used the word spirit instead of ghost, and I asked him why.

"I like the term 'spirit' better than ghost," he said. "To me, when you say spirit it's more believable than when you say ghost. Also, when you tell someone else about your experiences, I think it gives the listener the sense that the entity is a kind one and not threatening."

I tend to agree. Tell people ghost and most will immediately think of a scary or eerie being. The word spirit seems a bit softer and conjures up a kinder, gentler type of unseen occupant.

The first sighting involved a family friend who came to visit.

While entering the back door through the kitchen, the woman stopped and stared for several seconds. Jake noticed the reaction and asked her about it an hour later, over the dinner meal.

"Our friend told us she saw a beautiful woman, standing in the kitchen," he said. "She said the spirit was in her late 20s, had blond hair and wore a black full skirt with a white silk apron. Her hair was tied up in a tight bun. She said the spirit knew that our friend was watching, smiled to her and then walked down the back hallway—where the plate incident happened—and she disappeared."

Ellie and Jake explained that their friend who first saw the spirit is a well-known regional psychic, who has assisted police on difficult cases.

"A few years later, two friends were staying overnight during the Christmas holiday season," Jake said. "They were sleeping in one of the four bedrooms on the second floor. The woman said she woke up in the middle of the night and saw a female figure standing at the foot of her bed."

According to Ellie, the guest stared at the stranger but did not scream or become alarmed. She told her hosts the next day that the visitor had a calming effect on her.

"Here's the best part," Jake said. "This is an old house and difficult to heat. Since some rooms upstairs are pretty cold, we keep quilts at the foot of each bed. They're spread out so our guests don't have to ask for additional covers, in case they get cold. The woman told us the spirit moved close to the bed, smiled and said, 'I know you can see me, and I know you're cold.' Then she lifted up the quilt and covered our guest with it. Then she went out of the room through the closed door."

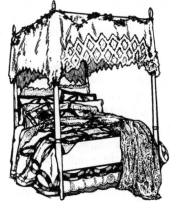

The next morning, the excited guest easily commanded the attention of everyone at the Christmas dinner as she told her tale and offered the same description of the spirit as was given by Ellie and Jack's psychic friend.

Jake said cold breezes leading to a specific room on the third floor make him believe that the spirit lives in the top level of the home, next door to the ballroom.

Another sighting involved Ellie's sister, Karen, who was visiting one week in the summer.

After a few days, everyone decided to take a ride to a local shopping center. As the car started to head out of the driveway, Karen shouted that she had forgotten her purse. While the rest of the afternoon shoppers waited in the car, she rushed into the house to retrieve her purse from the second-floor guest room.

Reaching the landing that led upstairs, Karen said she saw a woman at the top of the stairs. She described the stranger as young and beautiful with blond hair and wearing a full black skirt.

While Karen froze in place, the spirit smiled, turned and headed down the hall. Recovering from the shock, Karen rushed to the top of the stairs in time to see the stranger turn up the stairs to the third floor. When Karen reached the bottom of that set of steps, the spirit was gone.

"When she came back into the car," Ellie recalled, "she said, 'You'll never guess what I just saw!' Jake and I looked at each other as Karen told us about the spirit. Interestingly, my sister said that she never felt afraid and was very calm, more shocked or surprised than scared. That was the final time anyone has seen her, but you still get the feeling she's around."

"When I come downstairs at 5 o'clock in the morning," Jake said, "I get the sense someone is here, but I can't put my finger on it. Sometimes, I'll see a flash or motion from the corner of my eye, but nothing more than that. To tell you the truth, I'd love to see her. But I don't know if that will ever happen. It's been almost 10 years since the last sighting.

"The only other strange thing that sort of amazed me a few times," Jake added, "were the times that I passed the room where our overnight guest had heard the spirit talk to her. And, for one full week, or about that, every time I walked by that bedroom and looked in, the quilt was on the floor. It was as if something was dropping it there, for me to notice."

I explained that some people are unable to see the form of a spirit, but they are able to see the effects of its activity. Perhaps, that was what Jake was experiencing.

Suddenly, Ellie recalled another time that the spirit was seen. It was by the same psychic friend who initially spotted her.

One spring evening, Ellie and Jake were hosting a party in Rutledge House for the county arts organization, and there were about 80 people all over the first floor of the house. A group of women were standing in a circle, talking. Suddenly, one of them complained about how cold it was. Stepping back, another woman agreed, saying it was as if there was a frigid spot in the center of their chatting circle.

Off in the distance, the psychic friend who was there that evening saw the women move apart. The focus of her attention was the pretty young spirit in the black dress who was standing in the center of the circle.

"She told us," Jake said, "that the spirit seemed to be fascinated with a thin decorative piece of dead mink that one of the women was wearing around her shoulder. It was the kind that was all fur, but at the end there were the mink head and paws. The spirit couldn't figure out what it was, and she was trying to touch it." Laughing, Jake added, "That would make sense. Could you imagine someone from another time seeing this woman standing in the room, holding a drink and walking around with a dead animal hanging around her neck?"

"I think she likes parties and activity," Ellie said. "She seemed to be more active when the kids were here. Now, with all four of our children grown and gone, the house is a lot more quiet. She needs activity to get her going. I think that's why our friend saw her at the party, and I can only imagine how many times she's been here, standing around during other events, and no one was able to see her."

Two things still concern Ellie and Jake: They are disappointed that they haven't seen their spirit, and they are concerned about what will happen to her when they have to move away.

"We're both retired," Jake said. "We're going to get to the point where we'll have to move into a smaller place. I mean, not immediately, but eventually. I'd hate for this place to go to someone who would turn it into a lawyer's office or an insurance company. It's always been a home, a fun home with lots of laughter and parties. I'd feel a lot better if we were able to pass it on to another large, fun loving family."

"I just want to see her once, before we go," Ellie said. "I feel like I know her, and that she's satisfied with what we've done to her house. We're not spirit enthusiasts. But, even if we knew this place had a spirit in it, I think we still would have bought it, we loved the house that much."

Laughing, Jake added, "She's definitely here. She doesn't move furniture or lamps, she doesn't stomp on the floors or drag chains, but she's here. I mean, she actually talked to someone on the second floor. That's something you don't hear about every day."

Knowing their affection for the Rutledge House spirit, I told Jake and Ellie that some people believe that if you want a spirit to move to your next home you should place an open, empty box in the middle of the room and invite the spirit to come along.

"If I have no control over who moves in after us," Ellie said, "I'll get a box for her."

"Me, too," Jake said, "but I think she'd stay no matter who comes in next. This is really her house, and I don't think she'll ever leave here, even if she could. My greatest hope is that we can introduce her to a new happy family."

Slaves Forever

The character of the landscape changes near the northern tip of Delmarva. Smooth peninsula flatlands turn into rolling hills, and outcroppings of gray and white rock dot the wooded landscape. These stony formations add a dash of character to the edge of winding roadsides and accent knolls in the midst of barren farmland.

Archaeologists believe that some of these stony sites served as places for early American Indians' meetings and rituals. Later, settlers found these rock formations useful in making maps and directing those who would follow to new, unfamiliar locales. Some settlers built their homes near the most interesting rock patterns, which provided points of shelter and acted as natural sculptures in the yards of historic Colonial-era homes.

Today, some of these buildings and most of these rock formations still exist. This story takes place in Chester County, Pennsylvania, on a narrow road between Landenberg and New London, not far from the "Ticking Tomb" (featured in Vol. VII, *Up the Back Stairway*). While I cannot divulge the building's exact location, I will offer this brief description:

It's a stately home, nearly 250 years in age. It has been the residence of some noteworthy individuals. Constructed mainly of stone, it has four floors—including the attic and dirt-floored cellar. Several large chimneys jut through the roof in an irregular pattern. It has seen troops pass by its front porch during both the

11

American Revolution and Civil War, and, although it stands on a narrow road off the main routes to major regional cities, its silent spirit breathes history and, to a degree, horror.

This house and its owners have much to tell, but only some dare speak.

I met Angelique through Elaine, a friend with whom I used to work. She called and said I would definitely be interested in what Angelique, her coworker had to share. Over a bottle of wine one evening, the two legal secretaries for the same big-name Wilmington law firm somehow got onto the subject of ghost stories.

After listening to Elaine's experiences at a haunted beach house in Stone Harbor, New Jersey, Angelique began to recite a litany of unusual events that happened to her while growing up in the mid 1970s.

After a few phone calls, Angelique and I met in her Wilmington condo—no historic houses for her anymore. In her late 30s, the dark-haired professional who painted scenes of the Brandywine Valley in her spare time, shared a series of bizarre experiences that she and her family will never forget.

"It's still there," Angelique said, passing me a framed photograph of the 250-year-old Landenberg farmhouse. "There, under the side eaves," she said, as she pointed to a spot on the second floor, "was my room. Well, actually, I slept in a number of rooms during the eight years we lived there, but that was the last one I had. It was the one in which I felt the most comfortable. But, that's the end of the story. Let me start at the beginning."

Angelique's family moved in when she was 10. Everyone thought living in the country and on a small estate would be fun, a great experience for everyone. But things started happening on moving day, while the family was experiencing the bedlam that accompanied the transfer of belongings and bodies.

"It was broad daylight," she said. "You know what it's like, with people running back and forth from house to house, dropping off loads of stuff, and cars and trucks going in every direction. At one point, I was all alone in the house. I remember being on the second floor. All the floors were hardwood, so I heard a sound, like footsteps on the first level. I ran to the top of the main stairs, to see who was there. I thought someone had pulled up with another load of stuff, or a neighbor had come by to say hello. Then, I'll never forget this, at the bottom of the stairs, facing the steps, was a wooden chair with a TV sitting on it.

"Suddenly, the channel dial on the TV started to turn. You could see and hear it happen from where I was standing. Then, the chair started to move back and forth, like it was begin pulled aside and shoved back and forth by someone you couldn't see.

"I just watched and said to myself, 'Am I really seeing this?' It was broad daylight; not as if you just awakened or like you were in a state of altered consciousness. I don't remember if I told anyone about it at the time. I think I convinced myself I wasn't sure about what happened with the chair and TV and I let it go.

"But, things continued to happen. That house was so old. There was a huge amount of life and death stuff that happened there. Eventually, we discovered that we had more than one ghost."

Angelique said there was a ghost woman who stayed on the second floor. She could tell it was a female spirit because of the sounds of her footsteps on the wooden floors and also the swishing of the ghost's long skirts. Sometimes, the phantom passed so near 10-year-old Angelique that she said she could faintly feel the material of the dress.

Angelique also said that before they moved in there had been an outside porch that extended off the second floor of the house.

"On certain nights," she said, "you could hear voices and the sound of chairs rocking somewhere in the middle of the air, where the old porch used to be. This stuff happened all the time, but we learned one thing—there was safety in numbers. No one in the house ever wanted to be there alone. In fact, no one wanted to be in any section of the house by themselves. The thing that terrified me the most happened while I was working alone in the kitchen."

Angelique was making a batch of brownies. The counter was covered with cookbooks, a large glass jug of milk, big lumps of dough and a pan of melted butter, that she was stirring to pour into a larger bowl filled with the rest of the mixture.

"Suddenly, I couldn't move my hand," she recalled. "It was as if a force—like a spring or pressure working against two nearby magnets—was holding me back. I kept trying to force my hand against whatever it was that was holding it, but I couldn't move. Then I shouted, 'Would you just let me finish my cookies!' and I

13

had been pushing so hard that my hand suddenly flew forward and I almost lost the bowl. I said, 'Thank you.' But, within seconds, the metal lid on the milk jug came loose and started flipping up and down—making a 'blip—blip—blip—blip' sound. By now my adrenaline is pumping and, as soon as the milk lid stops, the lid to the toilet, in the bathroom off the kitchen, starts flopping up and down, with a louder 'blip—blip—blip' sound."

Another major incident happened the day Angelique and her mother were sitting in the kitchen with a man, who was in his mid-30s. Directly above them, on the second floor, was the catch-all room. Angelique described it as a place where all the extra boxes of belongings were left to be sorted out at a more convenient time. It also contained large pieces of furniture. There was one doorway into the room and two windows on the opposite wall. The door was closed but unlocked, and the two windows were fastened securely from the inside.

"It was early evening," she recalled, "still light outside. We were talking at the table when, suddenly, we all stopped and looked up at the ceiling. We heard all this stuff moving around upstairs. It sounded like someone was shoving boxes and furniture. We ran to the storeroom and found the door closed.

"My mother's friend, a big man over 6 foot tall, tried to push his way inside, but he couldn't get the door to budge. A few days later we got inside, and we found out that all the furniture and boxes had been shoved up against the door. But, it was impossible for anyone to do that, unless it could climb out the windows and lock them again, from the inside."

Angelique said the entire family had grown to hate the house. Acknowledging it was a scary place to live, her mother secured the services of a medium from Media, Pennsylvania.

"The lady went through the entire house with my mother," Angelique recalled. "All of us kids waited outside. She told us the woman on the second floor was kind, not evil. The medium explained that some people don't believe that there is anything after death. She said our second floor ghost didn't realize that there was more to her existence, and that she was disoriented. She was continuing her daily life, and she wasn't even aware of us being there. The medium said she was able to lead her to rest."

The other two spirits were a bit more persistent, Angelique said. The medium said they had been slaves, and that the woman was crazy and over time she drove the man insane.

"They were the ones who did all the stuff," Angelique said. "Things settled down a lot after the medium came through. But the activity never stopped completely."

Angelique accidentally found her haven in a room under the slope of the roof. Her mother also had used the area as a bedroom, but she had experienced quite a few eerie moments. Angelique said she found the room, which had its own wood stove, restful and she never had any problems at all.

"I used to play the kalimba, an African percussion instrument that resembled a thumb piano. I think that may be part of the reason that I never was bothered while I was in that room. Maybe playing the African instrument helped.

"There's another strange thing I remember," Angelique said, her face a bit flushed from her intensive stroll down Memory Lane. "God, I haven't thought about this for a long time, and all of these memories seem to be flooding back over me. Anyway, I had very long hair back then, and I lost my hairbrush. For a while I just borrowed brushes from everyone else. But, one day I woke up in my room and there was an old hairbrush—it had natural bristles and was odd looking, made of old-fashioned celluloid. It wasn't modern, even for the 1970s. Also, it wasn't any special day, like a birthday or anything, so I shouldn't have gotten any surprise gift or present. No one in the house admitted giving it to me, but I kept it for many years.

"When we moved, I took it to our new house in Newark, but I started experiencing strange dreams. I felt a strong presence, like something was trying to get inside me or live through me. Then I thought maybe there was a connection through the brush. I went out one night and buried it in the ground, in Newark, but far away from our new house. After that, I never had any problems."

Pausing, Angelique, closed her eyes a moment, then looked at me. Slowly, she added, "I imagine they're still there. The slave people and the older lady. If they are, that's truly amazing. Just think about it. It's probably been hundreds of years that they've been lost and wandering, not knowing how to go to the other side. Sometimes I get this idea that I'd like to go back inside there and look around, but then reality kicks in. You see, I'm actually afraid that they'd recognize me and might follow me back to my real home. I can't handle them again. Once is enough."

At the end of our conversation, Angelique looked different, obviously the result of recalling and, to an extent, reliving significant moments of those eight unusual years in the haunted farmhouse. I asked her what she thought of it all, if there was anything in particular she thinks she has learned from the experiences.

Laughing, she replied rather quickly, "That I will never, ever, live in an old house. Those years traumatized the whole family so that none of us—not my sister or my two brothers or I—has ever lived in an old home since. All of us are to the point now where we are able to choose where we can live, and we all have newer houses."

Author's note: A small business operates out of the building today. I spoke to an acquaintance who I know has worked in the building where Angelique lived with the three ghosts for eight years. I asked my friend if she had ever heard or seen anything unusual in the old haunted home in the country. "Oh, I never saw anything," she said rather quickly. "But I know that a lot of the people who worked there knew about the ghost stories, and they used to tease the new people. But it was mainly a private little joke. Except," she said, pausing, "no one wanted to work there at night, and no one ever wanted to be the last one to leave the building at the end of the day—including me."

Ghost in the Caroline County Jail

Ride through the central business district of Denton, Maryland, on a hot summer afternoon and it's easy to be captivated by its pleasant Southern Eastern Shore charm. Comfortable cafes and small shops along Market Street lead to the grassy lawn of the County Court House, easy to recognize because of its tall, white columns that frame the front doors of this classic hall of justice. A block away, over on Gay Street, stands the jail, Caroline County's central law enforcement outpost. Made of red brick, the large building presents a clean, safe, orderly appearance. Upon closer inspection, however, one can identify the oldest section of the building—the original jail that was erected in the early 1900s. To its sides and rear, are modern additions that have been built since the 1980s to respond to the county's increases in both population and crime.

Rambunctious locals who have been ordered to make periodic use of its cells, kitchen and recreational facilities refer to the jail as the "Waterfront Hotel," because of its location near the Choptank River. And some talk about the phantom prisoner that they or other prisoners or guards have seen, roaming the cells and also toying with the modern, high tech equipment.

To learn the stories about the jail's resident ghost, I met with former Caroline County Sheriff Louis C. Andrew, now age 71, who

17

served in office from 1961 until his retirement in 1994. He said he had been associated with county law enforcement almost his entire life. In 1938, at the age of 10, he moved with his family into the jail's residential area when his father—William E. Andrew—became sheriff .

Louis C. Andrew was appointed by Maryland Governor Millard Tawes to the sheriff's post in 1961, following the death of Louis' father, who had been county sheriff up to that time. Sheriff Louis Andrew was elected to eight consecutive terms as county sheriff—serving a total of 33 years. He lived in the jail-house building a total of 55 years, a portion of that time with his wife, Joyce, who helped her husband by cooking and feeding the prisoners.

"I lived there growing up," Louis said. "It was small in those days. Just like other jails on the Shore, the sheriff had to do the jail work and the other work, too, law enforcement. You did it all. It's different now."

"It was a 'Mom and Pop' jail," Joyce added, smiling, and her husband nodded thinking back for a moment of times long gone.

Today, he explained, corrections officers take care of all the prisoners and other officers carry out the law enforcement duties. But times have changed a lot since Louis Andrew's first years on the job—more people, more crime and different types of criminals and violations.

"Over the years, from 1961 to 1994," he recalled, "I had as few as one prisoner and as many as 103 at one time, but that larger number was after they added the new wing, after 1980. We'd have our county crime to deal with, and sometimes we'd hold federal prisoners for a period of time. You know, when they wanted to hide them somewhere for whatever reason.

"Back in 1961, it was basically disorderly conduct, drinking and theft. We'd have few murder cases, sometimes some trouble in the [migrant] labor camps. When I left in 1994, it was more rapes, murders. Drugs was a big thing, and we were still holding federal prisoners.

"It was a big change. In the old days, the daily base [of prisoners] would be eight to 12 a day. Then it went up to 20 to 24 a day, even before the 1980s. But that jail's a lot bigger now. A few additions have been built. The only thing left of the old place where we lived is in the front."

I asked the sheriff about the story of Wish Sheppard, the ghost of the jail

He said over the years there's been periodic interest in Sheppard's story, and even more interest in the ghost sightings of the former prisoner who, some say, haunts the Caroline County correctional facility even to this day.

Before he retired five years ago, the sheriff said senior high school students would interview him for their term papers about the Sheppard story, and they would ask to see areas in the jail where the sightings were said to have occurred.

But, he explained, all he could do is take them to the general areas where the haunted sites "used to be." Extensive interior remodeling has covered over the wall where Sheppard's hand print used to reappear, even after it was painted and plastered over. The old cells are gone, too, the ones where Sheppard was seen by both prisoners and guards.

But first a quick summary of the background.

In 1915, Wish (pronounced Wush) Sheppard, a black man, was found guilty of raping a white girl and sentenced to death. The wooden gallows was erected at the bottom of the hill, near the jail and along the Choptank River.

According to Sheriff Andrew, "There was a big crowd and people even came in boats to watch, and some others climbed up into the trees to see it."

Sheriff Andrew said he had talked with Sheriff James Temple, who was in charge of the Sheppard hanging. Temple told him there were three people up on the gallows with Wish, and they each put one hand on the lever. Then Temple came down with his hand and hit the top of the others, and that pushed the lever, causing the trap door to open and drop Wish through, sending him to his maker.

That way, Sheriff Andrew, explained, it was not just one man who was responsible for pushing the lever and doing the hanging.

Joyce Andrew provided me with a photocopy of a picture postcard taken at the time. A large mob of spectators can be seen crowding right up to the base of the tall gallows. Sheriff Temple and four other men are standing on the platform or steps of the death machine. Wish Sheppard is in the center with the rope around his neck—obviously just moments before he was to be hanged.

Unlike at today's hangings, no one was wearing a hood. And since the public was allowed to witness the execution—which also was a major social event—the townfolk turned out in force.

Somehow, Wish was able to leave a lasting impression on the cell wall that had been his last home here on Earth. According to Sheriff Andrew, the story is that when they came to escort Wish out to the gallows, he put up a struggle.

With one hand, he grabbed one of the jail cell's metal bars while he pressed his other hand against the cell wall.

'I did see that hand print," Sheriff said. "It looked like a man's palm and fingers pressed into the wall. We painted it over, plastered it over, and it always seemed to come back, and not too long a time later."

But, before telling me the stories, Sheriff Andrew added, "Now, let me say this," he stressed, "I've never seen anything strange in that jail, and I never experienced anything myself, no unusual sounds, no sightings, no stuff like that. All I can do is tell you what I heard from the prisoners and guards. I can tell you their stories, if they're of interest to you."

I explained that I understood his concern, and that I'd heard the same comment before. He was satisfied and, like a veteran storyteller, began to share a string of interesting stories about the ghost of Wish Sheppard in the Caroline County Jail.

"Over the years, the prisoners would always say somebody was in there," he said, "and that it was Wish Sheppard. They swore he was in there roaming around. One old fella, he was about 75 years old, he's dead now. He was a regular, in for disorderly. He always said there was no ghost in there, didn't believe it. One night, I went down to see how they were doing and there were seven or eight prisoners right up against the door. And the old fella was shouting, 'Sheriff! He's in here! I take it all back. He's in here. I seen him!'

"I went in there and looked around, and they followed me around like a bunch of little kids. They said, 'He went through that wall!' We used to have a real dark area, we used to call it the dungeon. I used to tell them, 'If you act up, I'll put you in the dungeon.' They didn't like that. You used to be able to get away with that in the old days. I throwed my light around down there and showed them there was nothing there, but they weren't satisfied. They were scared and said he showed up that night."

Another time, there was a man in the cell where Wish's hand print still decorated the wall. When Sheriff Andrew entered the cell area in the morning, the man said someone had come in during the night, took his watch and threw it outside, through an opening in the window.

"He had scratches all over his arm," the sheriff recalled, "from whatever it was was pulling on him. He was hollering and hopping around and said none of the other guys in the cell took it. He said it was outside. I went outside the jail and the watch was there, near the window."

The cell where Wish appeared was on the first floor of the jail building, the sheriff said. One evening when he had a pretty large number of prisoners, the sheriff was concerned that if there was a fire he wouldn't be able to hear the screams of the prisoners. To insure that someone could alert him by banging on a door that led to the offices, the sheriff locked one prisoner in the hallway, outside of the cells.

"It got so loud from him beating on the door," the sheriff said, "I went down and asked what was wrong. He said, 'Ya gotta lock me in the cell! He's here. Wish Sheppard. Ya gotta lock me inside with the others!' I opened the door and he jumped in. He was scared to death.

"A lot of the prisoners would hear footsteps, and not see him. They'll swing at him, but they can't hit nothing."

Joyce added an important piece of information, saying, "It was worse on rainy nights. It seemed they used to see him when it was raining. Now, I never saw or heard anything all the years we lived there. But I remember he'd go down to see what was going on and come back and say, 'Old Wish was down there again,' and I'd just laugh. I thought it was all a bunch of malarkey."

But the sheriff said he couldn't resist using the threat of Old Wish to quiet down the unruly prisoners from time to time.

"I'd tell them boys, 'It's a rainy night. You know who comes around on cloudy and rainy nights, don't you?' And right away, one or two of them who'd seen Wish would say, 'Sheriff knows what he's talkin' about,' and they'd quiet down."

One year, Sheriff Andrew had a woman in the jail for nine months awaiting trial for murder. He explained that he usually kept the women prisoners in the second floor cells. When he came in one morning, she said to the sheriff, "What are you trying to do, scare me?"

The sheriff replied that he wouldn't do that, and asked what she meant.

"Well," she said, "you pulled chains up and down the steel stairway last night."

Denying that he would even think of doing that, the sheriff said he knew the woman was serious. She had been in the jail for a long time, and they had gotten to know each other.

"I guess it was that Wish Sheppard," she said, seriously. "He was up and down with them chains all night."

Thinking back to that conversation, the sheriff said, "She swore she heard those chains. She was serious. But I never heard anything. Living in that jail as long as I did, I got up many a night, 'cause I could tell if there was something different or not right. But every noise I heard in that jail, I could explain. I never heard anything that was unreasonable.

"I had one psychic person come in. He came with some radio station, and he said he could tell things by vibrations. So he took hold of the cell door, and he said I can make out something is in there. Then he turned to me and said, 'Sheriff, you don't hear it because you don't believe. But I can tell you there's something here.' "

After 1980 and the renovations, the old cell doors were thrown away and the wall with the hand print was covered over. However, that didn't seem to get rid of the spirit of Wish Sheppard.

"I had guards tell me that the elevator would go up and down the floors by itself," the sheriff said. "They would tell me at 12 midnight, the elevator would come up, the door would open, they'd go and look inside and there was not a soul inside."

Sometimes, buzzers, that would summon the elevators would be sounding during the early morning. But, there was no one there to press the button, and it was protected behind an enclosed fence. So no one without a key could gain access.

A guard, who was out in the recreation yard, once told the sheriff that there was a figure pressing the buzzer on the third floor. But, when the guard got to the site, there was no one there—and no explanation for who or what it could have been.

"Another guard," Sheriff Andrew said, "he told me, 'I'm not kidding you, sheriff. I was in the control room and it was just a fog that come over me, inside the jail. And it just floated right through here.' He said it hit him right in the face, and he felt it. He believes it was Wish Sheppard."

Shaking his head a moment, Sheriff Andrew looked up at me and said, "I believe what I was told. I have to believe what they tell me. These are reliable people. People I trust. The other is just prisoners' talk. But, you have to understand that this is all of the stories that I was told. They all didn't happen at one time. All this happened over the years I was there. There wasn't something every single day."

According to an interview with Sheriff Andrews, printed in the book *Voices From the Land*, by Mary Anne Fleetwood, during construction the sheriff mentioned the ghost to members of the work crew. Soon afterwards the foreman told the sheriff not to say anything about Wish Sheppard's ghost or he wouldn't be able to keep his help.

Even after almost 85 years, the story of Wish Sheppard, hasn't been forgotten, mainly because of his ghostly visits.

On more than one occasion, Sheriff Andrew would be walking along Market Street and a friend or shopkeeper would call out a hello and ask, "How's ol' Wish doin'?", to which the sheriff would wave a hand and smile in reply.

"People knew about Wish," he said. "Prisoners talk. Word gets around."

And, apparently, so does the ghost of Wish Sheppard.

Friends Beyond the Grave

eidi lives in an attractive two-story, single home in a neat, quiet suburban community west of Salisbury. Now in her early 50s, she sat at a colonial-style kitchen table. Through the sliding glass doors was a pleasant view of her new spacious deck, with its large hot tub and vases filled with multi-colored summer flowers.

Sipping on a glass of iced tea, Heidi pushed back her reddish gold hair. Calmly, she recalled a series of unusual incidents that had occurred to her more than 15 years ago.

"I was about 35 at the time and lived in an apartment off Route 13, not too far out of town," Heidi said. "An older woman who worked at the desk next to me got very sick with cancer. It was bad, had spread to her liver, and she had to quit her job. I felt really sorry for her, and since I was living alone I sort of ended up taking care of her."

The friend's name was Gerta, and Heidi said the older woman was in her early 70s. After work and on weekends, Heidi would clean Gerta's apartment, do her shopping and take care of her aging dog.

"Gerta was from Germany and had no family or friends," Heidi recalled. "I was all she had, so I just sort of fell into being responsible for her. I also think she liked me because of my name, Heidi, which reminded Gerta of her friends in Germany when she was much younger."

As she stopped over to cook and visit and administer Gerta's medication, Heidi learned that Gerta's parents had been servants for one of the wealthy families in Salisbury. When they died, Gerta was left to get by on her own. One evening, Gerta asked Heidi to serve as executrix of her estate.

"I didn't have any choice," Heidi said. "Who else could she ask? I was the only one around. There were no other visitors or friends. I agreed, and I assumed she was as poor as a church mouse. I mean, she pinched pennies like nobody you know. When I went shopping for her, and the bill was $19.98, and she gave me $20, she expected me to give her back the two cents in change. I used to think she was crazy. I mean for two cents, it was annoying.

"Plus, her apartment was a total mess. She saved every scrap of paper, every receipt, every newspaper, every empty box. It was a disaster. I was not eager to get involved because I could sense it was going to be like that famous saying: No Good Deed Goes Unpunished."

Gerta told Heidi her conditions and dying requests.

•Gerta wanted her body donated to the local hospital for teaching purposes and research.

•There was to be no funeral service of any type.

•Heidi would have to promise to take care of Gerta's dog.

"I didn't like dogs," Heidi said. "Plus, this poor animal was old and deaf and blind, and it was a little yippee yappy dog. It would drive you crazy with its yapping voice."

But Heidi gave in. Soon after she agreed to Gerta's wishes, the older woman died a painful death at the local hospital. Heidi hired a lawyer and found, to her astonishment, that her poor friend, who looked like she didn't have an extra penny to her name, had a checking account containing more than $8,000. That, the lawyer said, was to go to Heidi.

A life insurance policy, valued at $10,000, was earmarked for the local animal humane society.

"The woman had put aside 10 grand for her dog!" Heidi said, recalling her astonishment. "And I had to convince them to take the animal, too. They were thinking of not doing it, but eventually they gave in and found a home for the poor thing. So I walked away with $8,000 and all of Gerta's possessions, most of which I trashed. The rest I sold through a local auction. I did keep a few items—some old furniture, a few pictures and knickknacks."

Heidi also arranged for her departed friend's body to be donated to the hospital for research. When everything was settled legally, she tried to move on and concentrate on getting her life back to normal.

"I started spending some of the money," Heidi said. "I got a VCR and bought some other things that were considered luxuries to me at the time. But, I had been good to Gerta and never asked her for anything at all. If she hadn't left me anything, it would have been fine with me."

About three months after Gerta had died, Heidi said she started waking up in the middle of the night, and each time there was a woman—staring at Heidi and dressed in an American Indian headdress.

"I couldn't see any features," she said, "but I just knew it was a woman. She had a calming effect on me. I wasn't scared. This happened every night for three full months, and many times she would appear up to three and four times in the same night. Sometimes, she would float across the room and go through the wall into the master bedroom. I figured it was Gerta. Don't ask me why I knew it, because the visitor didn't look like her at all. But it was, and I was okay with it. I'll also admit that at times it was a little annoying."

Still living in an apartment and dealing with her nightly phantom, Heidi decided she wanted to buy a home of her own. To help increase the amount of money in her savings account, she took in a boarder named Jill.

"Of course," Heidi said, smiling, "I didn't say a thing about Gerta. That would have been stupid. But about two weeks after she moved in, I passed Jill in the hall one night and asked how it was going.

"She stared at me sort of funny," Heidi recalled. "Then she said, 'To tell you the truth, the first weekend I was here I almost moved out.' Putting on my best I-am-so-shocked expression, I asked Jill why. And she said, 'The first night I stayed here, I woke up in the middle of the night. Something had grabbed hold of my feet and ankles. I didn't see anything, but whatever it was, it physically pulled me out of bed, over the footboard. I landed on the floor. I was grabbing the mattress and sheets, trying to hold on and stay in bed, but it didn't do any good. I just landed in a heap on the floor.'

"I asked her if she might have been dreaming, but she was sure that she was awake. I just said it was amazing, like I was totally surprised," Heidi recalled. "I also remember recalling that while she was sick Gerta had stayed in that room a few times. Thankfully, it never happened again, and Jill stayed with me for about a year. Eventually, I told her about Gerta, but I couldn't say anything about my ghost in the beginning or Jill would have flown out of there. To tell you the truth, I'm surprised she stayed. If someone grabbed my leg and tossed me to the floor, I would have been long gone."

On a few occasions, members of Heidi's family stayed in her home. They, too, saw the early morning visitor, but they were afraid to tell Heidi, because they didn't want to scare her. When the subject finally came into the open, they compared notes and realized they had all seen the same phantom.

Early one morning, after months of nightly visits, Heidi was awake in bed, sitting in pain from an infection in her thumb.

"It was throbbing and very painful, and that night Gerta didn't appear. I was so upset, I said to her out loud, 'All the time I took care of you, the least you could do is take care of me. Where are you when I'm in pain?'

"I was disappointed. I couldn't believe that I cared for her for so long and she wouldn't show up when I needed help. She wouldn't come out of hiding."

A week after the night of the throbbing thumb, Heidi received a call from the hospital that had received Gerta's body. The caller told Heidi that they were done with Gerta and they needed a decision on what to do with the remains—whether Heidi wanted them to hold a brief service or bury the body parts in an unmarked grave.

"I told them there was to be no service, and they were fine with that," she said. "But then I asked the man if he could tell me what period of time they had been using Gerta's body as a research vessel. And he said during the last three months, and they had just finished up with her about a week ago."

Heidi said all of Gerta's visits had taken place during the three months while she was being dissected and examined.

"I think she was at a state of unrest during those months," Heidi said. "I was probably the only person she knew that could make her feel safe. Maybe she needed somewhere to go to get away from the experiments. I don't know. But when she was visiting me, she didn't seem upset or angry. She was calm. I feel good about that, that she felt comfortable enough to come to me when she needed to.

"I never saw her again, ever," Heidi said, with a slight tone of longing in her voice. "I still think of her a lot. It was very odd when she was gone, not coming into my room each night. I wished she had come to see me in my new house. She only visited in the apartment, but she knew where that was, had been there, was familiar with the place. I do think about her, though. Some people say that when you think about them, they're nearby. I like to believe that, but I don't sense her here—not like before."

Iced In for the Night

Oftentimes, when I meet new people, someone will mention that I write ghost stories. When that occurs, a stranger usually will wait until I'm standing alone, come over and—in a whispered tone—offer to share his or her experience. Most of the time they'll say hesitantly, "But, only if you want to hear it." And I'll reply, quite honestly, "Sure!"

After all, I need to fill the pages of these books with new stories, and if people stopped sharing the unusual things that happen to them, I'd be in big trouble.

So, on this cool summer evening, Sherri and I moved away from the crowd surrounding the barbecue grill, grabbed two empty lawn chairs and picked out a spot under a distant tree—where she talked about the ghost she saw on an stormy winter night outside the city of Dover, Delaware.

A representative for a major clothing company, Sherri traveled up and down the East Coast. Her job was to visit shopping centers and malls to show off new merchandise. She explained that her company believed in hitting the grassroots department managers first and then her senior buyers would make a pitch at each company's corporate headquarters. Sherri's route included chain stores in malls located in northern Virginia, Annapolis, Salisbury, Dover, Newark and Wilmington.

During early winter, in January, an afternoon ice storm grounded Sherri in Dover. She spent the night in a motel room with her trainee who was accompanying Sherri on the route.

"It was a bad storm," she recalled. "The trees and streets were covered with ice and driving was horrible. The people at the store in the mall were really great. They arranged for us to stay at a small motel along the main road that cut right through town. There was no one on the roads. It was really a miracle that we were even able to reach the motel."

She said the place where they had to stay was of mid-level quality. Not as plush as a Hilton or Sheraton, but not a Motel 6 either. The name and site were unfamiliar, but she didn't care.

"Any port in a storm," Sherri said, smiling. "I was working with Cheryl, a trainee at the time. She's still with the company and we've become good friends," Sherri said. "Since we were inseparable at the time, people used to get us confused—you know, Sherri and Cheryl. It was an inside joke among the other reps. Anyway, we were given a room on the second level. We were exhausted and decided to call it an early night, so we didn't even watch the news and went to sleep about 10 o'clock."

The room had two double beds. Sherri was sleeping in the one farthest from the door and closest to the outside wall—near the windows. The curtains were drawn and the room was dark, except for a night light glow coming from the bathroom.

"Suddenly," Sherri said, "I woke up because Cheryl was screaming at the top of her lungs. It was 2 in the morning and she shouted there was an old woman standing near the bathroom door. I looked at Cheryl, who was wide awake and shaking. Now, I needed a few minutes to wake up, coming out of a deep sleep. I didn't see anything, so I tried to calm Cheryl down. I told her that it was probably a bad dream. But she just kept screaming. Next, I told her if she did really see someone it probably was the maid who came in early to make up the room.

"But she didn't want to hear it. She was sobbing and shaking under her covers. Also, the light on the night stand was on, and the door was unlocked and open, except for the chain lock. Neither of us remembered leaving it like that, and that really freaked us out."

Trying to act interested, but really wanting to get back to sleep, Sherri asked Cheryl what the woman looked like. Her friend described the middle-of-the-night intruder as "very old with white hair and no eyes, wearing a bright red glowing dress."

Then, with the light on in the room, and while Sherri was talking to Cheryl, the woman appeared again.

"I turned and there she was—with the wild hair and wearing the red dress," Sherri said. "She looked like a real person, not glowing or ghostly. I couldn't believe what was happening. And, in a flash, she exited the room. But she didn't disappear or go out the door, she floated in front of our beds and went out the window—right through the closed drapes into the outside—from our second-floor room.

"I jumped up and ran to look out the window, where she had gone through the wall and glass, but there was nothing. All you could see was the motel courtyard with the unused, covered over pool and all the cars coated with a thin sheet of ice.

"Meanwhile, my trainee is in hysterics. Cheryl was kicking all her covers off and screaming about the woman, or ghost or whatever she was. It took me at least 15 minutes to calm her down. I gave her water and soda. I didn't have any whiskey, but if I did I would have poured the whole bottle down her throat. I swear it.

"Needless to say, we turned on every light in the room. We were panicked and looked under the beds, in the closet and bathroom. We found nothing, thank God, and we stayed awake all night. In the morning, as early as we could, we got up and got dressed and were glad to get out of there. We didn't plan to say anything to the motel. They would think we were crazy and maybe call the police. It would only hold us up. But, when we approached the main desk, there was an argument going on in the lobby."

The first thing Sherri and Cheryl heard was a man yelling, "I don't care what you say. There was a woman in my room and she pulled my blankets off. Then she went through my wall, floated right through. And I wasn't drinking. I'm a Mormon, and I don't lie and I also know I wasn't dreaming. I didn't get any sleep all night, and I want a full refund."

Sherri and Cheryl moved closer to hear it all.

"We looked like we were up all night," she said, "and at this point I was getting upset, because the desk clerk was acting really ignorant to the older gentleman, treating him like he was crazy. So I excused myself and asked him what room he was in. It turned out he was in the room right below us, and the activity there had occurred at 2 o'clock, about the same time that Cheryl first noticed our visitor."

Sherri said the woman behind the registration desk became a bit more responsive when all three of the overnight guests started sharing ghost stories in the lobby. Several strangers passing by on their way to breakfast overheard parts of the conversation and a crowd started to form.

"Maybe this place is built over one of them Indian burial grounds," a man said, eager to hear more from Sherri, Cheryl and their new-found friend.

"Suddenly, a manager took us into the back office, away from the crowd," Sherri said, "and he offered to give all three of us a free night's stay, if we would just leave and not continue talking about the ghost. Cheryl and I agreed instantly. Even though our company was paying, we just wanted to get out of there and we were happy to dodge the paperwork and get on our way.

"But the man didn't accept the offer. He said he wanted to know the whole story, or else he was going to the newspaper. The manager, a middle-aged man with a bald head and beaten expression, told us he would share what he knew, but it wasn't much."

According to Sherri, he said a family was staying in the motel one winter about five or six years earlier. They had lived there for two weeks while the husband was out looking for work, but they didn't have much money and fell behind in their payments. Apparently, the manager or owner at the time got upset and threw them out—the husband and wife, two little girls and the grandmother. After they left, they drove around for a while, came back and parked their car in the rear of the hotel and left the engine and heater running. But, they had driven the rear end of their car into a mound of old snow and it clogged their exhaust pipe. The next morning, everyone was dead except the old lady. But she went crazy and they had to commit her to the state hospital. Since then, once or twice during the winter, someone staying in the section of the building where the family lived, reports that they've seen an old lady roaming the rooms.

The old man apparently was satisfied, got up and swore he would never be back.

"The manager just waved his hand, as if he'd heard the same response before," Sherri said. "To be honest, both Cheryl and I felt sorry for him. We thanked him for his understanding, but told him we wouldn't be back either. He said he understood, and we left. But, when we went back to the main office, Cheryl told everyone she met and word spread about our overnight adventure."

I asked her how she felt about that.

"In the beginning, I was a bit annoyed," Sherri said, "because some people thought we were crazy. Eventually, it didn't matter to me if they believed it or not. I could care less. I know what happened. I was there."

Since Dover was a regular stop on Sherri's route with new trainees, she continued to pass by the ghostly hotel.

"Each time I went by, I stared at the place," Sherri said, "but I never went back inside, even though the thought did pass through my mind occasionally. I wondered if it had happened again, and to how many more people. Then, one year, I drove up the road and it was gone. There was a restaurant there. The room where I stayed and the rest of the building had been torn down. I guess maybe that put the old woman to rest. I don't know. I haven't eaten in that restaurant, don't intend to. I would really freak if I looked up and she was walking out of the kitchen or happened to be my server."

I looked up at Sherri, and she was smiling, enjoying her joke.

"Seriously," she said, "even if the place doesn't exist anymore, I'll never forget that night and what she looked like. It wasn't just a view that happened in a flash. The woman was there long enough for me to stare right at her, to see her clothes, to see her go across the room and pass through a solid wall. She was human-like. I'll never forget the feelings I had while it was happening. She was ageless, I could not get a fix on how old she was. But that doesn't matter. All I know is she was there and we saw her.

"There is one other thing," Sherri said, explaining that the story of the old lady in the motel has become something of a company urban legend.

"One day, years after the incident," Sherri said, "another trainee and I were driving through Dover, and she turned to me and said, 'Did you ever hear that story about the ghost in the motel around here?' and I said, 'Yeah. I sure have. It happened to me!' And she immediately screamed with delight and wanted to know every detail of what had happened."

Agnes

Several sections of Woodstown, New Jersey, could serve quite easily as a setting for a Norman Rockwell painting. Its small town atmosphere makes an impression on visitors, even if they simply pass through on their journey to another destination. Distinctive downtown architecture complements nearby neighborhoods, which boast tree lined streets with ornately painted front porches and a healthy number of decorative and American flags.

This small Salem County community has it all—including, I've been told on several occasions, a fair number of ghosts.

I'd been promised at least a half-dozen stories about Woodstown's haunted houses, but none had materialized. That's not unusual; sometimes it takes time. But, in ghost hunting, patience is the name of the game.

Finally, on June 13 at the end of a book signing at the Richard Woodnutt House Bed and Breakfast in Salem (which has its own ghost, who is featured in Vol. V, *Presence in the Parlor*, of this series), Margie, a last-minute patron, arrived to buy a book and, more importantly, share her tale.

We sat in the upstairs parlor, only two doors away from the bedroom that hosts Sarah, the inn's resident spirit. While a late spring thunderstorm bellowed in the distance and rain pelted antique glass window panes, Margie recalled a series of unusual experiences in the early 1980s.

"My first husband and I lived in this old house in Woodstown," she said, "and it was haunted. I knew from the very beginning, but he thought I was crazy . . . at first."

A woman in her mid 40s, Margie continued, describing her former home as a "brick and frame structure built in the mid-1700s." The front, which probably had been constructed first, was made of red and tan brick. It was a small home—no fancy porch or turrets or secret passageways—situated on a moderate-sized lot not far from a picturesque lake.

"I loved that house," Margie said, seeming to conjure up a vision of the home in her mind. "But Travis, my husband at the time, he wasn't happy there. It was an older place, and it needed a lot of fixing up. From the very beginning, even before the activity started, I could tell he didn't like it. But, I'll tell you this, when our ghost started acting up and going after him, Travis hated it a lot more."

Soon after they had moved in, around November, Margie noticed that small things would be missing.

"They'd be there one minute, and then they'd be gone the next," she said. "I mean, just seconds later, and objects were missing. Then, during Christmas, we had these little decorative angels that were on the top of the tree. Suddenly, they just started flying around the room. My friends were there and they saw it, too. I knew something was up."

Active in the local historical society, Margie began to examine old records to discover the names of the home's former owners. While searching, she discovered there were several more "haunted houses" in Woodstown.

But, she told me with a knowing smile, "No one ever spoke about them, officially. They would pass by you and whisper about the haunted house stories," she added. "People don't discuss things like that openly; they only do it when no one else is around."

Apparently, Margie's home had a well-deserved reputation for being haunted.

"I know this," she said with conviction, "other people believed there was something going on in there. I love Halloween, so I decorated that house up and I thought it was fantastic. And, in all the years I lived there, no kids ever came to my house for trick or treat at Halloween. It was common knowledge that it was haunted."

One of the most unusual experiences in the home occurred immediately after Margie and Travis had finished a spirited argument. The topic of contention was the house. He wanted to sell it and move; Margie didn't.

"I was standing alone in the kitchen, and he was outside in the yard," Margie said. "Suddenly, the two wooden doors of the kitchen wall cabinet flew open, as if somebody pulled them apart. Then, five or six, heavy, stoneware dishes flew out across the room and smashed against the fireplace and broke into hundreds of pieces. It was almost as if someone was standing next to the cabinet and tossing the plates across the room."

I asked Margie what she did as this was happening.

"I just stood to the side and turned my body, so I wouldn't get hurt. Then, as soon as it stopped, I had an old table and chairs in the room, and they all started to shake and rumble up and down, on their own. I ran out and told Travis to get in here and see this. But, when he got inside the chairs had stopped shaking, and he said I threw the plates because I was mad at him."

Margie said she believed the ghost liked her but disliked her ex-husband.

"It was like it was there to protect me," Margie said. "I think whoever it was knew I was trying to take care of the house. I also believe that it didn't like him being there. So, I think the ghost decided to get rid of my husband."

Things would fly across the room and hit Travis. While shaving, his razor would be grabbed out of his hand and zip up the side of his face, leaving a cut on his skin. At other times, books would fly across the room and hit Travis in the legs or side.

"It got to the point where he wouldn't stay in the house," Margie said. "He'd just say, 'You can stay if you want to. I just don't feel comfortable here.' And he'd go spend the night at his parents' place. It upset him, but it really didn't bother me. I told him, 'I don't think the ghost will hurt you.'"

"Since there were so many little things happening," Margie said, "I kept a diary of everything that was going on in that house. The strange thing is, every time I got several pages done, the diary would disappear. Even after I've moved out of that house, and I've tried to write everything down again, each new diary disappears. I've gotten to the point where I've stopped trying to get it down on paper. I can remember it well enough. That's what's important."

Margie said the ghost would do silly things, just to make its presence known. She owned a cat-shaped puzzle with three removable letters. Often, the letter "A" would be missing from its proper place in the wooden holder, but it would show up later in an unusual spot in the house.

On several occasions, the toaster would disappear. But, in its place would be the letter "A" from the cat puzzle.

After returning from shopping one day, a large room-size rug was found rolled up and shoved in the hallway. During a Christmas party, there was an unexpected noise on the first floor. When Margie and friends went down to investigate, they found all the soda bottles lined up in a perfect row—but the plastic containers previously had been scattered on tables around the room.

Margie's ex-husband eventually contacted representatives at the parapsychology investigation center at Duke University. Several people came up to check out their house.

"They came with a secretary and a medium," Margie recalled. "They asked us to leave the house as they went through the entire building. Then they talked to us separately. The medium said she thought the ghost was a woman and that her name was Agnes. She said the ghost wore her hair pulled back in a bun—like I did at the time. She also liked to burn groupings of candles, which I also did and still do. The medium also said the ghost approved of some of the things we were doing to restore the house. And if there was anything she didn't like she would let us know. They wanted me to make an appointment to go to New York City, to be tested for my level of ESP. But I never went."

Armed with a name and confidence that she wasn't crazy, Margie traced the owners back to the days before the American Revolution. She also discovered the gravesite of the ghost's husband and son in an area cemetery.

Eventually, Margie was contacted by a descendant of Agnes. It was a young businesswoman who had been researching her family tree through the Mormon database in Salt Lake City, Utah.

Although she had settled in California, the young woman worked for an airline and was on the East Coast regularly on business. The next time she was in Philadelphia, she visited Margie in the ancestral home in Woodstown.

"She said she wanted to see the ghost," Margie recalled about the visit. "Unfortunately, for her, nothing happened all the time she was here. She stayed for several hours, and I walked her out to her car. When I came back into the house, I saw the letter "A" from the cat puzzle resting on the couch exactly where the girl had been sitting."

Responding to another memory from her haunted past, Margie said, suddenly, "She'd leave me notes." As if talking about a real life person, she continued, "I had a small tin of black, wooden letters—sort of like pieces from a Scrabble game. Sometimes I'd come downstairs and there would be a message spelled out on the counter. One time, I was supposed to take a plane trip to the West Coast. When I went through the kitchen, the letters spelled out 'Don't fly.' I called my husband and told him I wasn't coming.

"Another time, she took my car keys and left a note that said, 'Wait.' I called work and told them I thought my ghost had taken my car keys, and I would be late. They know about Agnes," Margie said, smiling. "Anyway, a half hour later than my usual time, I headed for work and passed a major accident at an intersection that I always used.

"For that reason, and other things she did, I always got the impression she wanted me to stay here and that she was protecting me."

Margie said she was fortunate to see Agnes a few times.

"One day I was in the bathroom, and I saw her, standing behind me. She was looking at me through the mirror. I turned quickly, but she was gone. It was a hazy figure, filmy, not clearly defined. But her clothing was old fashioned. Several other times, in different areas of the house, I could feel that she was nearby. If I turned quickly, I could see something move just out of my field of vision. My second husband saw a ghost in the same house. But it was a man—not Agnes. He said the ghost was standing beside his bed, and it was dressed in Victorian clothing. After a few seconds, it disappeared in thin air.

"Initially, he was like everyone else when you tell them your ghost stories. They just look at you with a stare, or they roll their eyes, like they think you're crazy. After that, he never questioned any of my stories again."

Over the years, Margie said she grew attached to her invisible housemate.

"I felt comfortable with her," Margie said. "I would talk to her, very comfortably. I asked if she wanted to come with me when I moved. I told her she was welcome. But I think she stayed behind."

Since she moved from that Woodstown home more than 15 years ago, Margie said she's often passed by her special haunted house.

"It meant a lot to me," she said. "I loved that house. In fact, when I got divorced, I was more upset about losing the house than getting a divorce. But, I've noticed nobody seems to own that house very long. It's always getting new owners.

"Also, it seems that everyone who lives there eventually gets a divorce. The people we bought it from got divorced. We did. The people who bought it from us also got divorced. In fact, I've heard there have been four people who've owned it since us and they're all divorced now.

"Sometimes, when I ride by, I feel like I want to go up and knock on the door and find out what I can. The house has been open on the Candlelight Tours, but every time I've planned to go in and visit, during an open house, something has come up to prevent me. I'm almost afraid to go there now."

Jinx House

They called it the "Jinx House," a modest, asbestos-shingled bungalow built among several dozen similar homes in a small Delaware County, Pennsylvania, development in the 1940s—during the height of World War II. According to my source, who once lived there, it's gone now. After reading this story, you'll probably ask, "Who would want to live in the 'Jinx House' anyway?"

I met Jason and Donna after the first Elkton Ghost Walk that I conducted with Historical Society of Cecil County historian Mike Dixon. Following the evening tour through downtown Elkton that ends under darkness in a Main Street graveyard, we returned to the society—housed in the former town library, which also is haunted.

While enjoying refreshments, Jason told me his strange story.

When he was 3 years old, on March 16, 1944, his mother was driving Jason and his sister through the Pennsylvania countryside. Jason's father, who was 29 years old, was operating a crane near Chester, at the Central Yard of the Sun Shipbuilding and Dry Dock Company, when he was crushed to death by the overhead tracks of the machinery. His body was rushed to the Chester Hospital.

According to the local newspaper, at approximately the same time, "The rear door of [Jason's mother's] car flew open sending Jason sprawling, tumbling, hurtling into the road. Distraught by the accident, they drove the baby to the Chester Hospital, where already in the accident ward, the family name had been written and marked out with death only minutes before."

In Jason's version, they rushed him into the emergency ward and put him on a bed. The doctor and nurse checked the nametag on his wrist and noticed that it was the same last name as the man—Jason's father—who had just been brought in dead and sent to the hospital morgue.

"There in the hospital," the paper states, "waiting for the doctor's' diagnosis of her small son's injuries," Jason's mother learned her husband was dead.

Apparently, Jason said, there were many people who believed the house where they lived played a significant role in the family's terrible streak of bad luck. He recalled hearing often about strange events associated with the home both before and after his family lived there.

In the newspaper story, entitled, "Man Killed in Shipyard at Moment When Young Son Falls From Mother's Car," the term "jinx house" competes with the bold headline.

"The story of the Jinx House," the newspaper story states, "unravels its plot grimly like the weird tale of a haunted house. The lot was purchased by a man, |who| before he built the house, was committed to the Norristown State Hospital. When the doors of that institution closed on the man, now healed of his mental illness, he returned to supervise the construction of the bungalow he planned to build."

But the first occupants moved away, sickened, neighbors said, by the effects of drainage that trickled into the basement of the home. The house remained empty for many months, until Jason's family moved in.

Initially, things were fine. But, within a few months, the entire, four-person family was hospitalized at the Chester Hospital with a strange flu.

"Again and again illness came," the newspaper states, "But Thursday morning, the sun was shining and it looked as if the Jinx House had lost its name. Thursday afternoon |following the father's death and son's accident| the name had come to stay."

Jason said he and his sister and mother eventually moved from the home. He said he believes that the next family was burned out by an unexplainable fire.

Today, there's an empty lot at the site. No one will build on it.

"They think it's built over an unmarked Indian burial ground," he said.

Perhaps the 1944 newspaper stated it the best, "The name that the neighbors gave the bungalow almost from the first time it was built is forever painted in the memory of all who saw the train of misfortunes which befell those who have lived there . . . The Jinx House."

Frequent Visitor

I moved slowly past the pair of concrete lions with dead eyes perched on two elevated stone columns. I was driving along a half-mile, tree-lined, cobblestone driveway at the northern edge of Delaware, not far from the Pennsylvania line. My destination was an office building, housed in a restored 1888 stonewalled, slate-roofed American castle.

Despite minor modern additions on the rear and left side of the large structure, the old mansion still had its turrets, gargoyles, jutting alcoves and large stained-glass windows—everything one would expect from the residence of an Old Country royal or haunted house.

Well, haunted office building now—since the last residential owners had moved out nearly 10 years earlier.

After brief introductions in the three-story foyer—complete with colorful banners and full-sized suits of armor—I followed my hostess, Faith, into her small but cozy office on the fourth floor. No elevator was present to spoil the historical ambiance, so the walk up four flights of wooden stairs was memorable, to say the least.

"Here we are," Faith said, as she proudly spread her arms apart and indicated the small suite where her ghostly experiences had occurred.

Odd-shaped windows looked down on the formal courtyard and nearby parking area. In the distance, an orchard, not yet in bloom, rose from a flat field and traveled over an adjacent hill.

43

In her main office was a cabinet with two closed doors that housed her books, plus a wide wooden bench, lots of plants and flowers and another antique wooden wall cabinet. This one, however, was modified to hold her personal computer, fax machine and copier.

A public relations executive with the company that I am not at liberty to name, Faith, pointed to the adjacent room, just outside her personal office space. "That's where all of the activity takes place," she said, directing my attention to the long, thin area that is used by her secretary, Jean.

"Since Jean is only here half a day, I spend the afternoons and early evenings alone, most of the time. That's when the activity occurs, when I'm here by myself, and only when I shut that door to my room."

During her first two years with the firm, Faith shared the suite with four other people. When an addition was completed, the rest of the administrators moved into the new wing, leaving her behind.

"That was a little over two years ago," she said. "I like it. I have my privacy, my own assistant, no distractions. I can get a lot done. But," she paused quickly and caught herself, then smiled at me and added, "I mean, there are some distractions. But I don't really mind him."

Him?

"Right, Him. I haven't given him a name, but he comes in here at least twice a month, but only since I've been working in here alone. And he won't do anything unless my door is shut and no one else is around."

Do what?

"Walking around, sitting in the chair. I'll be in my room," she said, "with the door shut at the end of the day, or early in the morning sometimes, and he'll come in." Faith got up and walked out into the hallway that led to the suite and showed me what she thinks happens—but has never seen.

"He'll walk through this entryway. I can tell because this old floor, right here, squeaks from the pressure when someone passes over this section. Then he sits down over there." Joan directed her body into the blue swivel chair behind her assistant's desk. "I can hear him sit in this chair, open and close the drawers, roll across the room and sometimes pick up the newspaper and rustle it as he begins to read."

Immediately after the first incident occurred, Faith told the president, but he told her not to worry, adding, "Practically everyone in the building had heard those old ghost stories," he said.

But Faith wasn't hearing stories, she was experiencing the real "unreal" thing.

"At first I would run out to see if one of my coworkers was here. In the mornings, my first thought was that someone else came in early. At the end of the day, I'd think someone else was staying late. But each time I rushed out to look, the room was empty. But I could sense someone was here. You just get that feeling, you know?"

I nodded. She continued.

"My sister is psychic, she can feel things. And my grandmother, down in North Carolina, she used to have a ghost in her house," Faith recalled. "She never would admit it or talk about it, though. But when we stayed with her, we heard footsteps at night and we saw the rocking chair move when no one was in it. So, I was aware of this sort of thing. It never bothered me and it still doesn't now."

After asking questions of the cleaning crew and other longtime employees, Faith discovered that an old tenant farmer and handyman, who was allowed to live in the section of the mansion that became her present office, had died in one of the rooms of her suite.

"He was here a few days before he was found," she said. "I guess after they carted him off, his spirit just didn't want to leave. He might have been a family worker who liked it here. It's fine with me. He seems like a friendly guy. He never bothers me, and I think he likes me being here and what I've done to the place. In fact, I feel safe and comfortable with him around."

I wondered if anyone else had seen or experienced Faith's invisible friend.

"Jane, my assistant, said the only thing she's noticed is that when she gets to her desk in the mornings, she finds her computer on a lot. She says she thinks he's into technology. But he hasn't left us any messages yet."

When I told Faith that some people give their ghosts names and talk to them, she shook her head firmly, indicating a definite no.

"I never wanted to disturb him, and he never disturbed me," she said, smiling. "I don't want to be too friendly. He goes about his business and I go about mine. Some of the other people here, the real old timers say they've heard voices in other parts of the building. The cleaning people usually work in twos on the upper floors. They don't like to come up here alone. I can understand that.

"One said that when he walks into my office he 'can smell death,' but I don't feel that way. I feel something warm and friendly is here, and I know it won't harm me. I like having my ghost around."

Deadly Violin

I n the fall of 1998, *Possessed Possessions* 2 had just been released, and I wasn't really interested in finding more stories about other haunted antiques, furniture and collectibles. After two books on the subject, I had decided to give that theme a break and concentrate on the balance of the *Spirits* series, but, there it was, on the top of the file—the small, green index card bearing Webster's name, address and telephone number.

I recalled the evening I had met him—a man in his late 40s with dark hair that crept well beyond his shirt collar. He also sported a lengthy beard—a bit unkempt, like the type worn by Appalachian mountain men—and on his feet was a pair of very pointed snakeskin, cowboy boots.

Even though two years have passed, the image of those boots is still easy for me to recall, especially since Webster was seated in the front row of the Port Penn Interpretive Center Museum on that mild April evening. With no one in front of him, the real estate salesman stretched out the two lengthy lower limbs of his tall body and consumed a good portion of my presentation area. I recall looking down and thinking that they reminded me of a pair of hefty logs that were erected to restrict my movement in the front of the small room.

It was after the evening's storytelling session, when most people had made their comments and drifted off, that Webster and his wife, Ginger, approached me and started to talk. I don't remember everything he said—there's often a bit of confusion with folks speaking in the background—except when he mentioned, "If you want a good strange story, and a true one, call me up about my haunted violin. It's a great one. Okay?"

"Okay!" I replied, marking down his name and number on the green index card—the same one that had gotten lost and then reappeared after *Possessed* 2 was written, published and out on store shelves.

Since a good story should never be ignored, I made the call and arranged to visit Webster and Ginger at their comfortable condo near Rehoboth, Delaware.

It was winter when I arrived and, in a cozy den—filled with hunting pictures of dogs and ducks—I listened as my hosts shared a most unusual and bothersome tale.

"Here it is," Webster said, tossing the black, fiber, violin-shaped case on the table.

"Don't put it there!" Ginger snapped. "I told you, I hate that damn thing. It gives me the creeps."

Rolling his eyes, he tossed his head in her direction, as if to say: *See what I have to deal with*, grabbed the handle and slid the case across the floor. With a small thud, it ended its brief trip and skid to a stop against the kitchen wall.

Sitting back down, Webster asked me if I was ready for the "whole story, or as much as I can remember."

I nodded and off he went, taking me back to 1983, when his 12-year-old daughter, Barbara, wanted to learn to play the violin.

"Why she wanted the violin, I'll never know," Webster said, tossing his arms up in the air. "We went through dance lessons, a year of voice lessons, even piano. Look," he paused pointing, "the damn instrument is still here, in the case near that wall. She doesn't want it now. Nobody plays it. But, at the time, we got her lessons, mainly because we already had this pretty good violin."

The instrument had belonged to Webster's father, who played for years and was quite good. The violin was stored in Webster's mother's home in Perth Amboy. After a few phone calls, his mother located the old instrument in the third-floor attic. Webster and Ginger drove up north, picked it up and returned to their South Jersey home.

"It was in pretty good shape," Ginger said, "if you consider the parts that were together. But, there were a few pieces that were rattling around inside the case. After we examined the violin very carefully, we thought it was worth fixing. Certainly, it was better and cheaper than buying a new one."

But it had to be fixed.

"Now, listen to this," Webster said, rolling his eyes toward the case. "The first guy I arranged to fix the violin died before I could even get it to him. At the time, it was no big deal—not to me, I mean. But, later, when things started happening, I figured that was the start of it all--the first sign that we let the monster out of the box."

I looked perplexed, but Webster assured me I would understand in short order.

The story continued.

When Webster started searching for a teacher, he discovered that violin instructors were nowhere as numerous as guitar teachers were. In fact, he said he probably could have located a tuba teacher with less aggravation. He also found it was equally difficult to find someone to repair the old instrument.

"Luckily," Webster said, "after a few months, I found a guy, living in a small town about 12 miles away from my job, who said he would give our daughter beginner's lessons. He also knew a guy up the road from him who repaired instruments in a shop out of his basement. So, I was lucky in finding two decent contacts to get the work done and start lessons."

While at work at his real estate office, Webster got a call that the violin was repaired. Grabbing his keys, he ran out the door and picked up the instrument in the middle of the day.

"Now, the things I'm telling you that happened after this are a bit strange," Webster said, "but I didn't notice it at the time, didn't put it all together until I looked back on the sad series of events."

When Webster returned to work, he brought the instrument into his office and left it on his desk. A coworker passed by, noticed the case and inquired about the violin.

"This female agent, only three desks over, was a musician," Webster said. "I didn't know it, but she played with a local community symphony. She asked to see the violin, so I opened the case. A few minutes later, she was sitting in the middle of the office, playing it for all of us for almost 45 minutes. She did a great job; she made really beautiful music. That weekend, she fell at home, broke her wrist and was unable to play or write for three months. She was out of business, just like that," Webster said, snapping his fingers.

"That was only number two," Ginger said, shaking her head and asking me if I wanted a haunted violin to take with me when I went home.

"But," Webster said, "like I told you, I didn't pay attention to it at the time. I just thought it was a tough break."

Later, Webster discovered that the broken wrist incident was just the beginning of a long string of bad luck.

Ginger picked up the story, recalling, "Our daughter only received two lessons from the violin teacher, because he got sick and died. That was very sudden and it bothered us quite a bit. Also," she added, "it was in early fall and we were unable to locate any other violin teacher, so we stuck the instrument in the closet and the lessons were done."

While the lessons ended, the bad luck lingered on.

A few weeks later, Webster learned that a major contact person—who sent him a steady stream of transfer business—had dried up. The person had been directed to send all new corporate transfer leads to a real estate agent in another office.

"That was a tragedy," Webster said, "and it just came out of the blue, with no warning. And, the bad thing was there really was no reason for it to happen, just bad luck or fate or something worse."

During a sudden ice storm a few weeks later, Webster was standing on his front porch. After looking at the landscape, he took two steps, to turn around and go back into the house, when he slipped and fell breaking his wrist and leg. He was out of work for four months.

"The only thing that helped us," Ginger said, "was that winter is not a real busy house buying season. He was ready to go back in the spring, but it was a difficult time—both financially and emotionally."

Getting up and walking to the window of the condo, Webster said, "While I was home recuperating, I had a lot of time to think. One thing that struck me was the number of accidents and worse that were associated with that damn violin. The woman who played it broke her wrist, the teacher died, I was injured and then lost my job.

"I was the top guy in the office, I had my routine and contacts established. Then, they pulled it all away, for no reason. I had to do phone duty, make cold calls and be thankful for whatever they would toss at me. I was in the business all those years, and it ended up like I was starting all over again, working with the new, entry level people. Essentially, I went from a career to a dead-end job. I decided that it was more than a string of coincidences. I decided that the damn thing was cursed."

Before I could reply or make a comment, Webster added, "I don't care if you think I'm crazy, what happened was more than abnormal. It was downright eerie."

Picking up the case, Webster brought it to the table and opened the lid. Within was a polished, dark brown instrument with bow. It looked peaceful and harmless to me. But it brought out a different reaction from Ginger.

"I told you, get that thing out of here. I hate it!" she said.

"Maybe he wants to pick it up, look it over," he said, looking at me.

"No thanks," I said, declining. "I've seen quite enough. You can pack it up."

Closing the lid but leaving the case on the table, Webster added one more piece of interesting information to the tale. For many years, his father used to play the violin.

"It was when I was much younger," Webster said. "I don't think I appreciated it too much at the time, as most children wouldn't. Apparently, he had considerable talent. This violin was the last one he played, and it had been sold to him by a man who was placed in a sanitarium."

According to Webster's mother, the man from the sanitarium had sent Webster's father a letter. In the correspondence, the man mentioned how sad, uncomfortable and depressed he was, living in the sanitarium.

"I just remember it was a plaintive letter," Webster said, "so full of depression. And this was the man who had sold the haunted instrument to my father. I have a feeling the violin also had something to do with my father getting

51

ill and dying of cancer. His serious illness started soon after he bought the violin."

Ginger shook her head and added, "He was in serious pain and it was a long and difficult illness. I also think the instrument had something to do with it. It's been closed up for nearly 15 years. No one wants it. No one will use it."

Apparently, the story of the troubled instrument has made the rounds in the family.

"I have a cousin who wants to play the violin," Webster said. "He lives up in Pennsylvania. But he says he won't come to see it, let alone touch it. I offered it to my nephew, whose daughter is interested in starting violin lessons, and he said he wouldn't touch it either. It's really a beautiful instrument, it just needs to be fixed a bit. There's a loose part that fell off. It's a shame it can't be played."

Looking again at the sleeping wooden musical piece, Ginger said, "It looks nice and peaceful there. You could take it to get it fixed and ready to play, but what good would it do if you got in an accident and died?"

Webster picked it up, pointed out the damaged area and said, "If I didn't have a sneaking suspicion that this is a demonic piece of some type, I'd be tempted to get it fixed again and learn to play it myself. I've always had an ambition to learn when I retired, but damn if I'm going to do that. I want it out of here before then."

Bargain Bed?

A reader of Possessed Possessions *1 and 2 who lives in Wisconsin had sent me an interesting letter about her "possessed bed." Following a lengthy phone interview in early May, I hung up the phone, turned to my wife and said, "Wait 'til you hear this one," and immediately got chills as I shared the highlights of a wonderfully eerie, bizarre tale from Middle America.*

Theresa, a factory receptionist and bookkeeper, lives in an old farmhouse in the country, several miles outside Green Bay, Wisconsin. One day Kate, her sister, arrived at Theresa's front door with an antique bed she had just bought at a charity auction held in the area.

"She knew I needed a bed for my 8-year-old son, Jeff,' Theresa said, "so she thought she'd surprise me and drop it off."

Theresa described it as "all metal, but paint chipped and rusted." According to Kate, the bed had been used at the old hospital in the early 1920s. It had thick exposed metal springs that caused the mattress to sit high off the floor. It only cost $20, a real bargain. Theresa had it sand blasted, repainted gray blue and placed it in the corner of Jeff's room.

"The first night he slept in it," Theresa recalled, "he had horrible nightmares. He woke up screaming that, 'The mean man was trying to get me!' It was very real to him. Initially, I thought it was the result of something he saw on TV."

53

After the nighttime disturbances continued for a week, Jeff's parents took him into their room and allowed him to sleep with them for a few nights.

"My husband said he'd get over it," Theresa said. "He said it was just his imagination and everything would be all right. While Jeff was in our bed, the nightmares stopped. But, when we put him back into his room, the bad dreams started all over again. Since they weren't as bad as in the beginning, we let Jeff stay in his room through the night. He'd wake up crying, but at least he wasn't screaming. He said he'd be okay, and I thought the worst was over."

A day or two later, while passing by Jeff's room, Theresa heard her son talking to someone.

"I went in and he was sitting in his room, on the floor during the daytime, and carrying on a conversation. But there was no one there. When I asked him who he was speaking to, he pointed to the bed and said, 'That man over there.' I thought it was just an imaginary friend. But I also thought it was odd that he would seem to be answering back to someone who was asking him questions. Another thing I noticed was that when Jeff was passing his room from another part of the house, he would stop and walk over to his door, shut it behind him and say, 'Good. Now the man can't get out.' "

Theresa told her husband about the string of unusual incidents, but she said, "He just said Jeff would get over it and it was no big deal. My husband's like that. He doesn't believe in strange happenings, unless he sees them for himself. To be honest, he thought I was crazy for being so concerned."

Things remained bearable until Theresa arrived at Jeff's babysitter after work and found her son screaming that he didn't want to go home, because "the man in my bed wants to kill me!"

"The babysitter was very concerned," Theresa said, "and I realized this was getting serious. I called my sister and she said maybe it was the result of the bed. And I thought—'Yes. It all started since the bed came, about three weeks before. I didn't do anything immediately, but kept that in the back of my mind."

One incident, however, caused Theresa to take dramatic action.

"The thing that creeped me up the most," she said, "was the night Jeff and I were on the living room floor, playing with his ABC cards. He was laughing and joking, and then, within a second, he started crying. When I asked him why, he pointed to the couch and said, 'That man over there said I'm stupid and don't know my ABCs.'

"I looked over, and I got this bad chill. And about as fast as I turned, I saw an indentation in the center cushion in the couch. Then, it filled up, as if someone has just stood up and took the pressure off the seat.

"I asked Jeff to describe the man, and he said he had 'scary eyes, weird hair and a lot of pimples on his back.' Then, he jumped up, ran toward his room and slammed the door, saying, 'Now he can't get out!' I just got the creeps and called my sister right away.

"She and a friend came over and took the mattress and the bed away. They wore thick gloves, and I don't blame them. I didn't want to even touch it. Just seeing it being taken out of the house gave me the creeps. But I was glad it was gone. It was about three and a half weeks that we had it.

"She lives on an old farm. They burned the mattress in a field behind her log house in the middle of the night. She told me it was eerie, gave her the creeps, too. They dumped the bedspring and frame in an abandoned silo. It's half below ground and all that's left of the barn and outbuildings, an eerie place at night. But that got rid of it. I'm glad it's on her property and not on ours."

Theresa said Jeff's emotional problems and all traces of fear disappeared immediately.

She described it as, "Just unreal. The very night we got rid of the bed, he turned into a completely different kid. He was himself again. When I think about it, I'm sort of mad at myself for not doing something sooner. It's scary to think this could happen. I told a few of my friends, the ones who wouldn't think I was crazy or laugh at me. They're just amazed at first, until I told them where my sister had bought the bed—at an auction at a closed down mental institution.

"I think whatever was inside that bed came here, and it was very evil. I'm not sure who was in it, or what area of the hospital the bed came from. It could have been used in a ward where they kept insane prisoners, or only God knows what. I really try not to think about who was in our house, living inside that bed.

"I can't even imagine what might have happened if I didn't get rid of it. One of the scariest things is the way Jeff described the man, with the pimples all over his back. That was a very unusual description and one a little boy wouldn't think up on his own. But, it's over now."

And what about Kate, Theresa's sister.

"She really believed it was haunted. She noticed, too, that my son wasn't the same, but when we got rid of the bed he was fine again. But there were two other strange things that happened. My sister also got a bed from that hospital, except hers was wooden. She said she started having dreams and she got rid of hers, too.

"This all happened in 1992. But, only about two years ago, my sister and our dad were outside her place, not far from the swamp, where she had burned that haunted mattress. There was still some of it left, and she said a huge snake came out of it and charged at them. It may have been a coincidence, but they said it kept hissing, trying to get at them. She tried to keep it back with the end of a garden hoe, but it didn't do any good. My dad went off and came back with an ax and chopped it up. He grew up in the country, and he said he'd never seen a snake act like that in his life."

Neighbor Talk

Ray and Sharon and their two daughters moved into their modern Cape Cod home five years ago, in early January immediately after the hectic Christmas and New Year's holiday season. They believed they were going to live in a dream house with spacious bedrooms, a basement with a playroom and a full-service country kitchen that Sharon loved from the moment they had first visited the open house several months earlier.

Moving day was exciting. The family traveled in three rented trucks from a small house within the city limits of Clayton, Delaware, to the new development in the suburbs of Cambridge, Maryland.

With the help of relatives and friends, they rushed to get all the boxes and furniture inside. Sorting things out would take some time, but that day's priority was to make sure each person's bed was set up, so they all could sleep comfortably that first night.

"It was a rough day, and we were really beat," Ray said. "We had the long drive down here from Delaware, then we had to unload three giant trucks. We wanted to get as much of the heavy stuff, especially the furniture, set up as soon as we could. I mean, we had the help and we figured we'd better use them while they were there. No telling if they'd ever come back. By about 9 o'clock, an hour after the help had finished up eating and left, we finally got the two girls settled in their new rooms. We've got two bedrooms up there. One was sleeping right above our heads. The other girl was on the same level, but in the far side of the house." Ray and Sharon were on the first floor, and they had the entire north section of the house to themselves.

About an hour after everyone was dead asleep, Sharon shook Ray and told him she heard noise coming from upstairs. Stirring from a sound sleep, he immediately heard footsteps and thought the children were fooling around and running back and forth between the two bedrooms.

"I ran to the bottom of the stairway and shouted up for them to settle down," Ray said, "but I got no answer. After a few seconds of silence, I heard the footsteps again. This made me really upset. I was dead tired from the move, and I just wanted to get a good night's rest. Plus, I just couldn't figure out how they could have enough energy to stay up, let alone play around up there. So I went up and looked around, but they both were asleep. I shut off the lights, went back downstairs and the damn footsteps started again. I ran up again, this time in the dark, hit the lights—and nothing."

Sharon said the sound of footsteps continued throughout the night, at least three or four more times. "Ray kept waking up and asking me, 'Did you hear that?' I did, but I wasn't going to go up and look around. I was getting scared by this time. As you can imagine, we didn't get much sleep that first night."

Nor for the next six nights, since the mysterious footsteps continued for an entire week. Sometimes they began at 11 p.m. and continued until 3 o'clock in the morning.

"This may sound crazy," Ray said, "but I was trying my best to explain what was going on. I tried to convince myself it was the house settling, or the doors creaking because they weren't level." Sharon agreed, "We even wrote down a list of possibilities, including the wind, tree branches hitting the house and things like mice in the walls. We didn't want to think or believe there was something spooky or ghostly going on."

At this point Ray said, "I believe in ghosts. In fact, I've lived in several haunted houses, so those things don't really bother me. What gets me upset is not knowing what's going on or why it's happening. Those unanswered questions or lack of reasons drive me crazy."

About four weeks after moving in, Ray was in the back section of his property, picking up dead tree limbs. It was early in February, and by this time the phantom footsteps were occurring only about three or four nights a week.

"A neighbor came over to the fence line," Ray said, "and he asked me how I liked the house. I said we were doing pretty good, but like any new place it would take some getting used to. Then I said the only thing that bothered me was the noises that sounded like footsteps on the second floor in the middle of the night. I also told him that my one daughter's room was really cold, the coldest spot in the whole house.

"Then he looked at me, shook his head and said, 'I shouldn't be telling you this, but you'll find out eventually. A man shot himself, committed suicide, in that cold bedroom you're talking about. I'm sorry to be the one to break the news, but somebody should have told you that before you bought the place.'"

Ray said he was in shock. He was more upset that the real estate agent had distorted the facts and said she thought that someone might have died in the home. Ray said he had lived in a house where someone had committed suicide before and he never had any problems there. This one, however, was different.

According to the neighbor, the young man, who was about 35 years old, found out he had a terminal illness. He left a note—warning his girlfriend not to come upstairs and to call 911. He taped it to the wall near the bottom of the stairway, then went up, locked his bedroom door and used a shotgun to blow off his head.

"The neighbor," Ray said, "told me the girlfriend ran into his house and then headed off in her car and nearly killed a couple driving down the road. My neighbor went inside and found the body, called the police and helped the medical team carry the corpse into the ambulance. He said there were bloody sheets and towels everywhere, and the cops and medics spread them out across the front lawn for evidence while they took pictures. The bad thing was a school bus filled with kids from the development rode by, and they all saw the cops and the bloody cloths. After that, the place was known as the Haunted House."

Ray told his wife the story after dinner, while the girls were upstairs. They decided to live with it and assumed that after a period of time their ghost would settle down.

"We figured that the move may have disturbed him," Sharon said. "Once we settled in, he would get used to us and everything would be fine."

After Ray's conversation with his neighbor, the footsteps continued, but they seemed less intense and also less frequent. However, activity of a different kind, this time directed toward Sharon's mother, moved the ghost back onto center stage.

"My mom was staying overnight and sleeping in the Cold Room, as we called it," Sharon said. "The next morning, she was sitting at breakfast and asked if anyone had walked into her room during the night. We said no. Then she said she thought she had seen a person standing near the side of her bed. Ray and I didn't reply, we just looked at each other and waited for more. Then she said that in the morning, while she was standing in front of the mirror combing her hair, she felt someone or something brush up against her. She said it was so hard that it almost knocked her off balance. At that point I called my sister."

Darcy, Sharon's older sister, had been studying the occult for years. She suggested Ray and Sharon leave their home and meet her to discuss their options. It was decided that Ray would have a serious conversation with the troubled spirit.

"What she suggested sounded reasonable," Ray said. "It was a sensible first step before calling in a priest to do a full scale exorcism. So I gave it a shot."

At midnight, on an evening when the two girls were staying with Aunt Darcy, Ray walked up into the Cold Room. In his left hand was a lighted blue candle. In his right hand was a blessed prayer book and rosary.

"I called out his name three or four times," Ray said, "and I got an ice cold feeling, like when all the hairs on the back of your neck stand up. I went to the coldest spot in the room, where my neighbor said he found the body. I said his name again, then I said something like this. 'We just moved here from Delaware, you know that probably. We intend to take good care of your home. We don't want any trouble. We don't want to hurt you or fight with you. I've got two little girls. They're good girls and we don't want them scared. We don't want anything to happen to them. You understand. I'm asking for your help. Please, go to rest and meet your family who are waiting for you, and just leave us be in peace.

"Then, all of the sudden," Ray said, recalling that night in the darkness of the death room, "the whole room got warm in a flash. It was weird, like somebody just sucked the chill of death away. And I said, 'Thank you,' and went downstairs and we haven't heard anything since."

Both Ray and Sharon said they're happy everything is over. The girls are comfortable in the home. They even had a birthday party for one of their daughters, and several of the children from school who were aware of the suicide still came over and had a good time.

"I knew there was something wrong here as soon as I heard the footsteps," Sharon said. "I went upstairs and found the cold spot in that one room, and I felt a presence there. It was odd. I knew that spot meant something, so when Ray came in after talking to our neighbor, I wasn't too surprised.

"But we've gotten through it. Things are calm now. And, if you think about it, no matter how annoying it was for those few months, we were better off than the man that killed himself."

Short Sightings

E*ach of the stories in this section is too short to fill an entire chapter but certainly too good to ignore.*

Still Kicking
New Castle County, Delaware

An emergency medical technician (EMT) was working on an ambulance run and dropped a dead body off at a local undertaker. A few hours later, the EMT was called back to the funeral parlor. While there he witnessed an event for which, to this day, he has found no logical explanation.

The dead body was stretched out on a long, stainless steel table in the undertaker's workroom.

As the EMT entered, the undertaker said, "Come with me. I want to show you something interesting, about that body you brought in a few hours ago."

Standing beside the corpse, the two men looked down on the lifeless body. The woman's eyes were closed, and a bright white sheet covered her body. An embalming flange protruded from the left side of her neck.

As the undertaker turned on the machine that fed embalming

fluid into the dead body, the dead woman's left hand moved up, heading for the side of her neck. He said it looked like she was trying to knock away the line carrying the embalming fluid into her body.

"She was flat line dead," the EMT said, recalling the memorable incident. "I'd seen movement before. Minor shifts in the body are normal after death. But this was different. When the undertaker shut the machine off, the woman's hand dropped back to her side. But, when he turned the embalming machine on again, the hand raised again and headed for the tube going into her neck. I turned to the undertaker and said, 'Is she dead or isn't she?'

"He said, 'In this world she's dead,' and he finished pumping her up. I'd say that was the strangest thing I've ever seen, and you see a lot of weird stuff in this job."

Visitors at Charlie Miller's Place
Newark, Delaware

When Todd was 18, he worked in the summer cutting grass at Welsh Tract Church, on the road of the same name south of Newark off Route 896.

"It was daytime, in the summer," he said, "and I was using a push mower, trying to get between those tombstones. It was hot, in July or August, so I sat down in the shade, under a tree.

Suddenly, I got the feeling that someone was behind me. When I got up and turned around, I saw two women, way in the back of the cemetery, standing over a grave."

Deciding to give them some privacy, Todd said he got up and went to the other side of the church overlooking the parking lot. But, when he noticed there were no cars near the church wall, he wondered how the women got there.

"I walked around to take another look at them," he said, "but when I got to the other side of the church, they were gone. There was no one there at all. Then I recalled that they were dressed in old-fashioned clothing, which was strange. I remember trying to logically explain how they got there and, more importantly, where they went or how they left without me seeing them.

"It didn't scare me," Todd said. "I actually thought I might have seen two ghosts. Today, thinking back on it, I can't think of any other explanation. They had to be ghosts, and I saw them, in the middle of a sunny day."

Author's note: The story of "Charlie Miller, the Headless Horseman of Welsh Tract Road," is featured in *Pulling Back the Curtain*, Vol. I of this series.

Up a Tree
Hartley, Delaware

While standing at the dock in Delaware City, a state worker in his early 20s and I struck up a conversation. When he found out I wrote books about ghosts, he said, casually, "I've seen a ghost."

"Tell me more," I said, pulling out a pen and grabbing an ever-ready notecard.

"I was out deer hunting one day," he said, "down on a farm near Hartley, west of Dover. And I was up in a deer stand, about 10 feet off the ground. I was watching for deer and I saw an Indian come walking through the woods.

"He was dressed in skins and had a feather in his head, and he was carrying a bow, with the arrow in the string, ready to shoot. I just watched him, for about a few minutes. He was hunting deer, too. Then, he looked up at me and raised his finger to his lips, as if to tell me to be quiet.

"I just kept watching and then he started to move in a direction, toward a thicket. Then, two or three deer jumped up and ran off. When I looked back at the Indian, he was gone. Disappeared. But he was there. I saw him.

"Went home. Told my father. He acted like he wasn't surprised. I'll never forget it. That was really something."

Non-returnable Gown
Raleigh, North Carolina

A young woman called me when I was interviewed during a morning program on WDCG-FM in Raleigh, North Carolina. The focus was haunted objects featured in our two books on *Possessed Possessions*. She said she had bought a Victorian era wedding dress at an antique shop in a quaint North Carolina town.

"It was an unbelievable gown at a truly unbelievable price," she said. I told her that I would bet there were some spirited strings attached to her "bargain."

She agreed, laughing nervously as she shared the rest of her story.

The first night she took it home, she hung the large dress in her bathroom and turned on the hot water in the shower—to steam out the wrinkles. A while later, the bride-to-be was awakened by a rustling sound. Following the noise, she opened the bathroom door, hit the light switch and saw her gown waving back and forth—but there was no open window and no reason the garment should have been moving.

"That bothered me a little," she said. "But, the next night, soon after midnight, I awoke when I heard the sound of something hitting the bottom of my bathtub. When I went in and checked, I saw a button from the dress had fallen off and caused the noise. The next day I sewed it back on before I went to work, and I put the dress back in the bathroom, hanging it where it had been."

That night, she heard the button sound again. Checking, the woman found two buttons resting in her bathtub.

"I was really upset by this time," she recalled, "and I decided the gown was bad luck. I mean, I don't like this kind of stuff. So I tossed it in a trash bin on my way to work. And that night, a little after midnight of course, I heard the same rustling sound. I was really freaked, so I opened the bathroom door and the gown was hanging there, right where it had been for the previous three nights."

Terrified and frantic, she called her boyfriend and he came over. They took scissors and, on her apartment floor in the middle of the night, they slashed and cut the dress to shreds and tossed it in a trash box in her kitchen. The next morning, the gown was undamaged and resting across her breakfast table chair.

"I was really shaking," she said. "I knew I had to get rid of it. My boyfriend said we should try to burn it. But we lived in the city. What were we going to do? I didn't have a fireplace. And we couldn't go into the park and put it in a can and light it. People would think we were crazy for sure. The only thing I could think of was getting it to the nearest antique shop and letting somebody else have it. I could care less where it went or who was stuck with it, just as long as it didn't come back to me. And, thank God, it never did."

The DJ thanked the caller, but before she hung up, she added to the story.

"There's one more thing, though. I got married, but it didn't last long. Only a few months. He had a lot of problems. Sometimes, thinking back on that gown, I wonder if it was trying to warn me. It may sound crazy, but no crazier than what happened while I had it."

Happy Birthday!
Pitman, New Jersey

As I was heading toward Fort Delaware aboard the *Delafort*, a New Jersey resident asked if I wanted to hear his ghost story.

In his home in Pitman, he had suspected there was something unusual. He had heard footsteps, saw blurred figures passing to his side. But, he could never focus on anything that was substantive, that made him feel very firmly that he had witnessed a sighting or a genuine bizarre event . . . until his daughter's birthday party.

As the festivities were winding down, the children moved to play games outside and he found himself alone in the house. Turning on the television, he settled in to watch a Phillies game.

Suddenly, an orange helium balloon, with a long dangling ribbon, moved past his field of vision. Pausing, he watched the rubber, air-filled toy travel around the room and head out into the hall. Getting up, he followed the balloon as it passed through the hall, up the stairs out of sight, and then, a few moments later, came back down and settled in the central hall.

I asked the man what he thought.

"I didn't know what to think," he replied. "I only know that it was impossible that it could happen on its own. It couldn't just go from room to room, because we have walls coming down from the ceiling, creating doorways. The thing, actually, would hit the wall, move down until it got under the door frame, and then guide itself into the next room, and into the hall and then up and down the stairs. And if it was a breeze blowing the balloon, it would only go in one direction, not maneuver around the walls and hallways.

"It was as if some invisible thing—a kid or person or ghost—was pulling it along and down and wandering with it through half of the house."

Wisely, he never told the story to his young daughter and her friends that day. But he kept an eye on the balloon for the next few days.

"It eventually died on the floor on the first level of the house," he said. "The gas seeped out of it, just like with any other balloon like that. But, I'll never forget how it went from room to room. It was impossible, but it happened."

Disappearing Graveyard
Southeastern, Pennsylvania

A University of Delaware faculty member stopped me on the way to work one morning and mentioned he enjoyed searching graveyards. One of his hobbies was locating unusual tombstones and the final resting places of the famous and infamous.

Over the next few minutes, we exchanged interesting tombstone inscriptions and shared directions to "must see" cemeteries in the Mid-Atlantic region. I directed him to several local sites, including the famous Feb. 30th tombstone in St. Peter's Church Cemetery in Lewes, Delaware, and a grave marker carved in the shape of the state of Delaware in a graveyard outside Clayton, Delaware, both included in "Tombstone Tales," featured in Vol. II, *Opening the Door.*

Before departing, he offered an interesting experience he had while seeking a final resting place in southeast Pennsylvania.

"There was a local photographer who went up north and found an unusual cemetery," he said. "All of the gravestones had the way a person died carved and listed, in addition to the person's name and date of death. I thought the article and pictures were interesting," he added, "so my wife and I took a trip to locate the spot and look at these unusual stones."

When he arrived in the town, he could not find the cemetery.

Frustrated, he stopped the car and ran into a small store, seeking a native's assistance and directions to the graveyard.

"The woman was very helpful," he said, "but she told me, 'We used to have a real nice little graveyard in town, until some photographer came up here and published his pictures of our graves in the paper. Then, somebody came up here and stole all our gravestones.' "

Keep in Touch
Tangier Island, Virginia

Patricia and Carol were best friends from the time they were born on the island. They attended school and grew up and played together, were in each other's wedding parties and were the closest of friends for their entire lives.

While in high school, the two girls made a special promise that when one of them died, the other friend would come back and let the living person know what it was like after death. Over the years, they discussed the promise and they both vowed to keep it beyond the grave.

While in her 40s, Patricia died suddenly of blood poisoning, and Carol never forgot her friend. She'd think about Patricia often. They had been together so much that there wasn't a place on the entire island where Carol could go that she hadn't been there at some time with her best friend.

There were hundreds of memories that Carol couldn't discard, and she worked so very hard to keep Patricia alive in her thoughts.

One day, while ironing in her kitchen, Carol felt a cold chill crawl up the back of her neck. It was late and a few minutes later she closed up her ironing board and headed up to bed.

While climbing the stairs, Carol knew Patricia was trying to contact her. That evening, in the middle of the night, Carol awoke and saw Patricia standing at the foot of the bed.

Her friend was hovering above the edge of the wooden footboard. Carol said she knew she was awake and not dreaming because she looked at the clock beside her bed and it read 2:10.

"I saw Patricia smiling at me," Carol said, recalling the visit. "Then I heard her say, 'I came back like I promised.' And I said, 'I know, now please leave. I'm frightened,' and Patricia disappeared.

"I know it was her," Carol added. "But I didn't want her to stay. It was amazing that she was able to keep our promise, but she wasn't supposed to be with me. She belonged on the other side, and I think telling her to go was the right thing to do."

Skull Face
Fort Delaware, Pea Patch Island

In May 7, 1999, my friends Ron and Annette, who had taken the Fort Delaware Ghost Tour before, brought along two first-timers to the haunted island. As Dale Fetzer was performing in the Commandant's Office in the refurbished Administration Building, I waited outside in the fort's courtyard.

It was getting dark. Cannonballs were rolling, creating a thunder-like sound. A few resident bats were out, adding to the evening's eerie atmosphere.

Suddenly, one of Ron and Annette's friends rushed from the building, seeking me out.

"You won't believe this," he said, visibly shaken and distressed.

I waited for more.

Almost stuttering, the man explained that he had seen a "skull," looking at him from a framed photograph.

At first, I thought he was toying with me, seeing if I'd believe his bizarre story. But this wasn't the first time that people had seen unusual things on the ghost tours. (The year before, a young woman was terrified—and wanted to leave the tour—after seeing a Confederate ghost who, she said, passed right next to her arm.)

I followed the man inside the building and watched as his shaking hand pointed toward the picture of Zachary Taylor, dressed in a dark military uniform.

"There it is," he whispered, trying to not draw the attention of the other 90 ghost seekers. "I swear, I saw a skull. It was right there, for three or four seconds. I just froze, then I closed my eyes and looked again, and it was still there. I couldn't believe it. The third time I looked, it was gone. But I swear it was there. It was a white skull, with two eyes looking right at me."

As Dale Fetzer completed his presentation, a large group gathered around the nervous member of the evening's tour. And, as has happened quite frequently, word of mouth spread another unexplained story that has been added to the Ghost Lantern Tours of Fort Delaware.

Ghost of Old County Road
Glasgow, Delaware

J.J. was driving east on Old County Road, from Maryland into Delaware about 2 o'clock in the morning. It's a narrow, winding, secluded route, an area where you would never want your car to break down. Suddenly, he saw a man standing in the middle of the road.

"One minute the road was empty and clear, and the next second, there was a guy in the road—just staring straight at me. It was definitely a guy," J.J. said. "He scared me, I'll tell you. I was only 18, and I wondered what I should do. If he didn't move I was going to hit him. If I stopped, I thought he could mug me, or kill me and take my car. I took my eyes off the road for just a second, to see if anyone was behind me, and when I looked back at the road in front of me, he was gone. No one was there."

J.J. said the man was wearing blue jeans and a red shirt. He was right in the middle of the area illuminated by the car's headlights. Without slowing down, J.J. drove right over the spot where the man had been standing and headed quickly toward home in Newark.

"I had already decided to keep on going, not stop no matter what," he said, "but that whole experience was weird. I didn't tell anything about it to anyone. I didn't want people to think I was crazy or drinking or anything."

A month later, he was riding late at night along the same stretch of Old County Road with his friend George at the wheel. About two miles before they reached the spot where J.J. had seen the ghostly figure, he mentioned the sighting to his friend.

"He went pale," J.J. said of his friend George. "Then he told me, 'I'll show you exactly where you saw this guy.' And he stopped the car at the exact spot where I had seen the figure. George told me he had seen the same thing, wearing the same colored clothing, but he never told anyone because he was afraid people would think he was crazy. We both laughed about it, real nervous like, and drove off."

71

About a month later, while driving with his brother, J.J. was tuning the radio as they approached the state boundary line on Old County Road. Suddenly, J.J.'s brother screamed that he saw a figure of a man in the middle of the road.

"That makes three sightings," J.J. said. "By then, everybody in my family had heard about the Ghost on Old County Road—we gave it a name. But the strange thing is that my mother has a friend who lives right near that spot. She told my mother that she used to have an old barrel or oil drum in her backyard, but it was stolen."

So?

"A few months later," J.J. said, "that barrel was fished out of the Chesapeake & Delaware Canal, and inside was a dead body."

J.J.'s theory is that the ghostly figure belonged to the man in the barrel, who had been run over on the road at that spot. Scared, his killer found the metal barrel, stuffed the dead man inside and tossed it in the nearby waterway.

"Maybe he appeared there until they found his body and buried him," J.J. said. "I don't know. I guess it's as good an explanation as any. But every time I drive down that road, I look for him. I have to admit, I don't use that road as often as I could. It still gives me the creeps, and I never drive it by myself."

I Know the Place
New Castle, Delaware

While at a book signing in Fair Hill Antiques, north of Elkton, a man came in and told me he had an experience—back in the 1970s—in an apartment on the third floor of an old mansion in New Castle, Delaware.

"For the first three or four weeks, my new wife and I would wake up in the middle of the night," he said. "Doors would open so often that we had to nail one of them shut. They just wouldn't stay closed."

His wife, he said, would always feel like there was someone else nearby. One night, he was awakened by his screaming wife, who was shouting, "Would you just leave us alone!"

"I asked her, 'Who are you talking too?' But, the strange thing is, she didn't know. She said, 'I have no idea.' After that, things settled down, and it never happened again. But that was a strange place. What do you think of that?"

I smiled and said, "I bet I can tell you where it was."

The man looked a little amused, and he said, "Go ahead, give it a try."

"I bet you were living in the old mansion with the five-story tower on Seventh Street, that's now known as Fox Lodge at Lesley Manor."

Astonished, he asked how I knew.

When I told him stories of the inn were in Vol. V, *Presence in the Parlor* of our series, he bought a copy to take home to his wife. No doubt, that night they read about the other haunts that occurred in their old residence—and they knew they weren't crazy at all.

Watchful One
Cape Charles, Virginia

Marge opened a small day-care center in her home. One night, about 6 p.m., near closing time when there were only two young children left in the building awaiting their parents, she walked into the playroom and saw an older woman watching the children.

Careful not to scare the youngsters, Marge smiled at the stranger, who looked up and returned the friendly gesture.

"It didn't seem as if the children had seen the old woman," Marge said. "So I didn't make a big deal out of it. But, as soon as their mother picked them up, I was shaking. I watched the old woman for about two or three minutes in the room before she disappeared. I wouldn't leave the children alone the minute I saw the stranger in there. She looked like she was enjoying the children. I didn't know who she was, but I got the sense that she wasn't going to do anyone any harm."

Marge said she knew the stranger was a ghost the minute she saw the woman. The apparition had a glow about her and she could only be seen from the waist up.

"When my husband got home, I told him what happened," she said. "Then my hair really stood up on the back of my neck. 'Cause he told me he had been seeing the same thing, in the day care and in other parts of the house, for some time. He told me he was afraid to tell me about it. He said the old lady smiles, like she's a pleasant person who enjoys the company of the children. I admit that I was afraid at first. Now, though, whenever I see her, which only happens a few times a year, it doesn't bother me any more."

Gravity Hill and the Ghostly Grave
Franklin Lakes and Parsippany, New Jersey

Rebecca lives in northern New Jersey, but she is majoring in art at the University of Delaware. During a conversation, she asked if I had ever heard the story of "Gravity Hill." I said I knew it was somewhere in upstate New Jersey, but I had not visited the site.

"Well," she said, "I've been there, and believe me it's for real."

During the next 20 minutes, she shared her experiences at two popular haunted sites in the Garden State. Gravity Road, or Gravity Hill as it's also called, is located in Franklin Lakes—in the northern part of New Jersey not far from the New York border—at the Ewing Street exit of Route 208.

"There's a legend," Rebecca said, "that a young girl was killed on the road, at the bottom. If you drive there and you shut your car off, she'll push it backwards up the hill. But you have to be careful and only do it late at night or real early in the morning, when there's no traffic—'cause you go backwards, the wrong way up the road. The cops will give you a ticket if they catch you doing it. So you have to look out the back window a lot, in case someone else comes driving along and you have to turn your car back on and drive off."

One summer night, Rebecca and a few friends drove to the site. She was with a friend in his pickup truck and the other couple was in a Mustang. Rebecca and her friend got to the bottom of the hill, shut off the truck and left it in neutral. Her friends did the same thing to their car, which was about 10 feet in front of the truck.

"It was freaky," she said. "It really started moving, back up the hill. My friend wasn't touching anything except the steering wheel. I was really freaking out. You have to steer the car, because it's moving on its own. But, that night, the truck was moving slower than the Mustang in front of us. It was going so fast, backwards, that it was going to hit us, so we had to turn the truck on and drive out of the way. It was amazing. I couldn't believe it, couldn't believe my friend wasn't touching his car. We went there expecting it to be nothing, like really lame, and it was, like, exactly like everyone said."

That same night, the two cars drove to Parsippany, New Jersey, along the back roads several miles off Route 46 to a quiet churchyard in the middle of the country.

"We were just hanging out, talking about weird things," Rebecca said, "and someone suggested we should, like, go see the Glowing Grave. We'd heard stories about it, so we said, 'Whatever,' and headed out to have some fun."

When they arrived, the four friends got out of their cars.

"I was freaked out," Rebecca said. "You could see this gravestone glowing, from a good distance away. It was, like, glowing and there were no lights anywhere nearby. There was nothing shining on it. I was so scared. It like really spooked me out. It was really freaky. I'll never forget it.

"I'd go back, but never alone. No way. I wouldn't do Gravity Hill alone either."

Piece of the Past
Newark, Delaware

Melody admitted that she shouldn't have done it, but she couldn't resist the impulse. *After all, it was the Haunted Dorm,* she thought. *And how cool would it be to take a few bricks from the basement of the scariest building on campus back to my room and use them for doorstops or decorations.*

So she took them. And then it happened.

"It was the most frightening dream I ever had," she said, waving her hands across the front of her body, as if she was trying to push the feeling away, to keep it from coming back.

"I woke up in the middle of the night, and I couldn't move. I was totally frozen in place. I remember thinking, *Just move the leg, and then the arm*. But nothing would work. I looked straight at the clock. for 10 long minutes, fading in and out of sleep. Then, finally, I was able to get up, grab the bricks and run them outside and toss them onto the grass near the sidewalk."

I asked Melody how she knew it was the bricks that caused her fearful frozen state. It could have been anything from a bad meal to plain bad luck.

Calmly, she said, "The man in my dream, the young, good looking guy with the T-shirt told me to take them back, to get rid of them. But he didn't actually say those words. It was more like he was talking to me without vocalizing. Instead, he was sending silent messages, thoughts. It's hard to explain."

I wondered if she had gone back to the building and returned her haunted contraband.

"No," she said, shaking her head. "I'm afraid to go back alone, and I can't really tell my roommate that I brought haunted bricks into our place on purpose. So I'm going to let them stay outside for a while. Maybe, if I'm lucky, somebody else will come by and want them and take them away. Yeah. That would be the best way to take care of it."

Uncle Chuck
Pocomoke City, Maryland

Uncle Chuck was dying of cancer. It was painful for his relatives to watch him fade away, his body only a dwindling image of the strong man that Uncle Chuck used to be.

The older man lived with Marty, his nephew, and Judy, Marty's wife.

"He used to go crazy if anyone left his bedroom door open," Marty said. "Uncle Chuck didn't want anyone to see him in his sickly condition. After he died, we had him cremated. That was his request. He also said he wanted his ashes scattered under the tree in our front yard, where he always liked to sit. We did this, even though I didn't think it was the best place to sprinkle his remains. But, it was one of his last requests, so we honored it."

The night of the funeral, about 8 o'clock, Marty and Judy started to clean out Uncle Chuck's old car. It was a 1970-something, copper-colored Plymouth Fury, a huge old boat in excellent mechanical condition. However, it needed a fair amount of body work. When the engine fired up, Marty recalled, the Fury sounded like several motorcycle engines needing mufflers were driving through the neighborhood.

When they were done with the car a few hours later, Marty put a "For Sale" sign in the front windshield. That night, he left the car facing the street, hoping a passing buyer would notice the fine example of classic American-built transportation and take it off their hands.

"The next night," Marty said to me, "this is really crazy, so get yourself prepared. When we started going through my uncle's papers in his room, the car started up. It was sitting under his favorite tree. The car doors were locked; the ignition key was in the house in the kitchen drawer. No one could have gotten into the car, but it started up on its own. The lights went on, and it actually moved about 10 feet, from under the tree—with no driver and stopped by itself.

"I hurried out to the car, got inside, checked the brakes and shut off the lights. There was nothing else I could do. I moved it back, but instead of parking it under the tree, I drove it to the far end of the driveway, got out and locked it up—again. This time, it was fine for the rest of the night."

While that was the end of the unusual events connected to Uncle Chuck's car, it apparently wasn't the end of spirited Uncle Chuck himself.

A few nights after his bedroom had been cleaned out and his car sold, Marty and June heard noise coming from the old tree in the front yard.

"I looked out the window and saw a ghost standing there," Marty said, "right where I had sprinkled Uncle Chuck's ashes, like he asked me to do. I watched the ghost for about a full minute, and then it disappeared.

"I really think it was Uncle Chuck," Marty said, seriously, "and he came back to say good-bye, and to let me know that I had done a good job caring for him and taking care of all of his final arrangements. I was never scared. He wasn't the kind of person who would hurt you. Even when he was sick, you knew it was the illness making him upset and angry, so why should he try to hurt you after he was dead?

"For all these years, I never told anybody this story, because my wife said people would think we're crazy and put us in a place where they keep the insane. But I know what I saw, and there's nothing that can change that, ever."

Pretty in Pink

I n all my travels, I've never been able to find this particular
house, but the story was told to me by two people, from
opposite ends of Delmarva. So, I believe there must be something to the tale. If anyone knows where this house is—or was—
I'd be thrilled to hear more.

As the story goes, a young, recently married man named
Henry was the perfect husband—trustworthy, polite, always in
good humor and totally responsive to his beautiful wife, Francine.
She, on the other hand, was overly demanding, openly abusive
and constantly curt. Basically, she was Cecil County's early 1900's
version of the "Wicked Witch of the West."

No matter what Henry did, it was never enough.

Everything Francine said was correct, and everything she pro-
posed was a good idea.

Everyone who lived near their home, and others who dwelled
for miles in all directions, knew the two persons were locked in a
strained relationship. But, it also was obvious that Henry took the
abuse well. He was never cross, never raised his voice to question
his wife, never corrected her—at least in public—and through
every valley and rut in their marriage he maintained a steady,
calm, reliable appearance.

But, each person has a breaking point, and everyone wondered when Henry would reach his.

While his wife was away on vacation with her mother, Henry arranged to have their grand Victorian home repainted. It was to be a surprise for Francine when she returned.

Henry took delight in the project, directing the three painters, helping where necessary and enjoying their efforts as if he were performing the brushwork himself. As always, he complimented them for their work and, at the end of the job, he gave them a healthy bonus. On the day Francine was to arrive home, Henry stood at the front gate, dressed in his Sunday best, to greet his wife and mother-in-law as they disembarked from their carriage. A few neighbors, who had just finished praising Henry for a "job well done," waited nearby.

But, instead of accolades, Henry received arrows. Francine screamed that he had ruined her house, that she hated the color, that he had no right to make such a decision without her. "Everyone in town knows pink is my color!" she shouted. "This house has always been pink, and pink it shall remain!"

Henry stood motionless, a soulless human statue, a beaten man flogged once again on what should have been the day of his greatest triumph. The pathetic porch scene at the Pink House was described in every saloon, church meeting and grange hall in the county. Henry, the tellers said, was serving his Hell on Earth. Francine, on the other hand, was a heartless, ruthless witch, who was lucky to have chosen such an understanding—or gutless— husband.

Two weeks after the embarrassing incident, neighbors noticed that Henry was repainting the house—in pink, of course. But this time he hadn't hired any help. He was doing the job alone.

To those few who dared ask, he explained that he wanted to have it done before Francine returned from her latest trip, and it was important that he do it himself, to make up for his past fail- ures.

It took young Henry three weeks to finish their home, but finally the Pink House was back in the pink.

Neighbors waited in anticipation of Francine's arrival. One local merchant was holding bets as to whether the town's resident shrew would praise or scold her husband.

But, Francine didn't return.

Two months turned into three. Eventually, six months passed, and the Cecil County countess never appeared.

Henry provided the authorities with as much information as he knew. She had traveled alone to Cape May, New Jersey, for a few weeks of rest at the ocean. He knew nothing more.

No one expected Henry to be upset. To be honest, all the neighbors and most of the townfolk were happy for him. At least he was at peace. Word spread that Francine had run off with a banker from New York City and was living in a grand estate near Central Park. Another story circulated that she was in New Orleans, the wife of the owner of a fleet of trading ships.

Laughing, one Cecil County resident said, "Whether she's in New York, Balt'mer or Hell, the poor devil she's taken up with has his hands full, that's for sure."

As time passed and he lived on his own, Henry started to exhibit a new found confidence. During the next several years, he became quite the extrovert, waving to passers-by, laughing and partying with his neighbors, speaking of his bright future. He worked every day, was active in his church and never remarried.

For the next 25 years of his life, no one ever heard him say that he missed Francine—and why should he?

She was never very far away.

After Henry died, his attorney released the contents of a letter directing his executor to purchase a modest gravestone for Francine. It also left instructions that her remains, which he had buried 25 years earlier in the root cellar of their home, be placed beside him in the town cemetery.

There also was information of a most interesting nature, explaining that Henry had used Francine's blood to make the perfect blend of her favorite color—pink—that he had applied with zest to her Pink House.

And those who continue to tell the tale say that Henry and Francine's home still stands, somewhere in Cecil County. They also believe that the special mix of perfect pink rests beneath a layer or two of more modern colors—waiting to be discovered and unleash Francine's evil spirit on a new generation of helpless men.

Battle of Meadow Park

Sandy rushed a glance at her watch. As usual, she was running late. The tiny voice in the back of her mind reminded her to get to the Acme in the Big Elk Mall as soon as possible, to get Ted's shrimp.

They were on sale for two days only, "Jumbos at $5.99/lb. Limited supply!" the flier announced.

Ted loved all kinds of seafood, but shrimp was his favorite. But they had to be jumbos, had to be steamed at home, and they had to be ready the minute he sat down at the table. "No waiting at home for me," he told Sandy. "Not like in those damn all-you-can eat places where they get ya in, take your hard-earned money and then make ya wait forever. A man's home is his castle, and me, I'm the king."

She'd heard that expression hundreds—no thousands—of times during their four years together. She could tell it was coming by the expression on Ted's face. Sometimes, when in a daring mood, she would turn her back to him and mouth the "castle and king" part silently, in unison with his voice. But, she'd never do it to his face.

That had only happened once. And once was enough.

As she raced past the bathroom, Sandy stopped, reversed her direction, and jumped inside. She couldn't delay much longer. If she was late and they were out of jumbos, Ted would go crazy. But she was afraid to leave the house without one last check—to make sure nothing showed.

The weather was miserable inside the trailer and out. Nothing new, just another hot and humid July Saturday at the top of Delmarva. With perspiration forming on her upper lip and several beads of sweat dripping down her forehead, she adjusted the scarf around her neck—tied it tighter to make sure it wouldn't slip—then ran out of the trailer.

Both windows were down in her 10-year-old Chevy Nova as the 21-year-old slim, red-headed woman headed east on Route 40. The car was a moving furnace, but she concentrated on the relief of the air conditioned supermarket.

Sandy planned to spend as much time inside as she dared. Ted wouldn't be back from his fishing trip off Turkey Point for six more hours. That gave her time to get his shrimp and window shop at Peebles, where she'd look at nice things she would never be able to buy.

It wasn't like this in the beginning, she told herself, waiting at the red light at the intersection that led to North East. She stared through the steaming windshield as smiling couples and families towed their boats south toward the Head of the Bay. The Pennsylvania Navy, locals called them. But, Sandy thought, at least they're together, having fun, not fighting.

The scarf was cutting into her neck. She shoved a finger beneath the red material, trying to get some relief, when the tip of a nail accidentally rubbed against the raw spot—the dime-sized red blister caused by Ted's burning cigarette.

As Sandy pulled her finger loose, a pair of tears fell and mixed with the sweat dripping down her chin, back and chest. The light changed and an impatient driver, comfortable in his refrigerated foreign sportswear, nudged her with a long blast of his horn.

Sandy hit the pedal and raced toward the store. There, for a few hours, she could hide. Be safe. Try to forget the biggest mistake of her life.

She had been happy in Scranton, Pennsylvania, was doing well in her first two years of high school. She had a few good friends and enjoyed living with her grandfather. But, at 17, with no parents, no siblings and only a male grandparent to answer to, she started to drift away, stay out a bit later than usual, skip church and, in general, show off her rebellious teenage spirit.

Ted said he was visiting the area for a few days to do some hunting and fishing. He and Sandy met accidentally at a convenience store when they literally bumped into each other at the gas pumps.

A brief conversation led to a dinner meeting, and that evening they spent the night together in the next town. When he left the area, Ted promised to write—and he did.

He said he was a successful salesman with a nice house near Baltimore—"Where there's dancing and parties every night, and I've got lots of money to take care of you forever."

Weekly letters turned into daily phone calls. After a second secret meeting, Sandy took off with her jewelry box, one suitcase and the balance of her savings account.

She left a note for Grandpa Jack, the 60-year-old, retired coal miner and widower who'd taken care of her since her parents' death in a car crash when she was six. "Thanks for putting up with me," she wrote. "But, this town's too small for me now that I've grown up, and I've found the perfect man. I'll write when I can. Love. Sandy."

But she never wrote.

She wanted to, but at first she just couldn't find the time. Later, she was too embarrassed and too scared.

Ted, it turned out, wasn't perfect. Within three months, Sandy's Mister Right had broken her nose, finished off her bank account and gotten her a fastfood job supporting him and his taste for hard liquor. It was nine months after she left, while she was thinking of going back home, when a high school friend sent her the news clipping. Grandpa Jack had died.

He didn't own much—no car, just a few pieces of beat-up furniture in his rented house. There was nothing for her but the unmailed letter—written a week before his heart attack—that was found in the old man's dresser.

Dear Sandy,

I'm real sorry I let you down. Your parents probably died 1,000 times, looking down from Heaven seeing how I was unable to help you, when you needed it the most.

I was never no good with younger people. Your grandmother should of lived longer. She should of been the one here to take care of you. Then, all this would probably of been lots better. But, God left me behind and I guess I messed it all up pretty good. I hope you're happy with your man. That's all I can do, now. Wish you well.

I don't have nothing to send you. No money. No present, only good wishes and some prayers. But, I tell you this, if you ever need me, need my help, I'll do what I can. Just call me. Reverse the charges, and I'll fix it so you can come back home.

I guess that's it for now. Love you,
Grandpa Jack

When Sandy first read the letter she clutched it to her chest, kept it tight in her fist, not wanting anyone else to see it, touch it, know what it said. As she cried and rocked on the floor of Ted's rusted, run down trailer, she pictured her grandfather. She saw his strong hands, his white beard and the pale blue and black lines that crept across his forehead and down the left side of his face—marks from the coal dust that had seeped into his body when he was trapped below, in a cave-in while in his 30s. She still remembered how he would say, "Every day I look in that mirror, I wonder why the hell I'm not dead. Why God let me crawl out, when so many others died down in that hole. I guess He wasn't done with me yet."

❖   ❖   ❖   ❖

As she ordered Ted's shrimp, Sandy's mind went over what she had gotten out of the relationship—one broken arm, three concussions, several blackened eyes, a smashed nose, five lost teeth and 17 cigarette burns—counting the one on her neck that Ted had given her the previous night, for not having fresh batteries for the TV remote.

Slowly guiding her cart through the cool Acme aisles, Sandy looked at food she would have liked to buy. But, even though she paid the bills, the "king of the castle" decided who would eat what, and when.

The fresh burn under her scarf felt better in the chilly air. Sometimes she pretended she was living with someone else, anyone else. She'd look at men—walking alone along the street, or at others passing in trucks and cars—and she'd wonder which one beat his wife or burned his girlfriend with cigarettes and then threatened to kill her if she told anyone or approached the battered women's shelter or police.

That's why she stayed—out of ice cold, red hot fear. She knew most people would think she was crazy for not running away, but most people would never experience Ted's terrifying abuse.

"Ya ever try to leave me," he once told Sandy as he shoved the cold metal barrel of a dark pistol into her mouth, "and I'll slice ya up and toss your ugly body in the bay. If they ever find ya, all they'll get is a hunk of bloated meat and a hundred crabs enjoyin' a free seafood buffet."

Ever since she received the letter, Sandy prayed to Grandpa Jack each day. She'd repeat the same message—asking forgiveness for running off, and praying that he'd talk to God and somehow make her life better. She knew what she did was wrong, but she figured she had paid enough by now. And, if she decided to kill Ted in his sleep, she didn't want to burn in hell.

Saturday night had gone well. Ted enjoyed his shrimp, polished off seven cans of Natty Bo and passed out in the old hammock strung between a telephone pole and the backside of the trailer.

On Sunday morning, Ted was up early, dressing in his uniform. A member of the 15th Pennsylvania Volunteers, he was excited about the Civil War re-enactment that day at Meadow Park. If Sandy were asked Ted's three favorite things, she would say drinking himself into oblivion, kicking her in the ribs and dressing up as a Civil War Yankee—in that order.

"How do I look, Babe?" he asked her, smiling at his Billy Yank twin in the bathroom mirror.

"Wonderful, honey," Sandy said, encouraging him to leave so she could enjoy a few hours of safety. Plus, she knew Ted was into re-enacting because he could punch and kick anyone within reach to his heart's content. Several guys from other units who had been hurt by him had sworn to even the score, and Sandy wasn't eager to watch a scene that often turned bloody and ugly. Besides, she had made plans for later that afternoon.

"Ya wanna come and watch?" he asked, offering to let her sit in the blazing sun for three hours and wave at him.

"No, thanks. I've got to clean up from last night and . . . ."

Snarling, he snapped and turned, pressing his face into hers. "Whatdaya mean by that? Like I'm some kinda pig that messed the place up last night?"

"No," Sandy said, shaking. "I just meant that I have to stay and clean . . . ."

"Yeah! Ya haveta clean is RIGHT! Look at this dump. If ya kept up with it, ya wouldn't have to do it now, and ya could come and watch me kill a buncha Rebs. But, no! Other guys'll have their babes there, but not me!" Ted's voice took on a sing-song tone as he grabbed her long red hair and pulled Sandy toward the trailer's floor. "So, stay here, then. But this place better be perfect when I get home, or I'll give ya a matching birthmark on the other side of your neck."

As Ted's gleaming black boots stomped out the door, Sandy huddled on the floor and cried, trying to decide which was the most painless way to commit suicide.

The Battle of Meadow Park was nothing like the major re-enactments held at Bull Run, Gettysburg or Sharpsburg. Since there had never been a Civil War engagement in Cecil County, the town commissioners decided to manufacture one to boost tourism and let locals who were members of nearby units show off for the hometown crowd.

A few hundred enthusiastic spectators surrounded the field. Dozens of barbecue grills sent off columns of white smoke, carrying the smell of ribs, hotdogs and hamburgers among the battle watchers.

With about 80 Yanks and 130 Rebs lined up at opposite ends of the field, someone shouted "CHARGE!"

As friends and family applauded and re-enactors howled war cries, the sweating, wool-uniformed men advanced in two irregular columns under the hot July sun.

From a limb in an oak tree about eight feet above the ground, Sandy picked Ted from among the crowd of blue coated soldiers.

She aimed the barrel of her .22 caliber rifle at Ted's head.

Back home in Pennsylvania, she had spent her summers shooting rats as they crawled from the abandoned mines toward her grandfather's garden. If she could take out a rat's eye at 200 feet, she figured she'd have no problem hitting the side of Ted's head. He wouldn't feel a thing as her bullet collided with his brain. And, with so much confusion and gunfire caused by the re-enactors blank cartridges, no one would notice that he had been shot for real until the imitation battle was over.

Sandy clicked off the safety and, slowly, she took up the slack. Her finger made contact with the trigger.

On the field, a Rebel officer shouted to the stranger beside him. "What outfit you with, Mudsill," using a re-enactor term for low-life. But the older man remained focused, smoking his cigar and charging with the rest of the swiftly moving line. His face showed he was determined to meet the attacking Yanks and drive them from the field of battle.

Sandy followed Ted with her dark metal sight, waiting for just the right moment.

Another re-enactor farther down the line shouted at the same man, "We're gonna kick some Yank butt, right, Hog Rubber?" letting fly another Civil War insult.

Again, the stranger didn't response, continuing to press forward, the thick, dark cigar clenched between his yellow, jagged teeth.

Sandy could sense her chance would come soon. She would have to be careful, catch Ted at the moment when he was standing alone, away from anyone else.

Now, only 10 feet from the enemy, the 200 soldiers prepared for hand-to-hand battle. As the swaying lines met, bedlam erupted as 20th-century Yanks and Rebs tossed down their muskets and scores of grown men wrestled like out-of-control schoolboys.

The old stranger scanned the enemy, gliding through the confusion, moving like a cat, avoiding rolling bodies and fist fights that went beyond the planned script.

He had a score to settle. Smiling, he spotted his target up ahead—12 . . . 8 . . . only 4 feet away—dressed in dark blue and laughing as he smashed his gleaming black boot into the thigh of a small, 10-year-old Rebel drummer boy.

"TED!" the old man shouted.

Sandy's "king" paused as his eyes tried to locate the caller.

It was the right moment, and Sandy pulled the trigger. But Ted abruptly took a step to one side, responding to a call from someone along the battleline.

"HERE!" Ted replied, looking around and seeing a bearded man approaching at surprising speed.

The bullet passed less than an inch from his ear and sank harmlessly into the Meadow Park grass. Sandy cursed and crawled down the tree. Shaking, she shoved the rifle into a baby carriage that contained a sleeping doll, and rushed toward her car. She was upset that her one chance was gone, and she wanted to be prepared for Ted when he came home—drunk, bruised and in an angry mood, as usual.

On the battlefield, Ted found himself flat on his back against the ground, pinned by the incredible strength of the old stranger whose lips were pressed against the Yank's ears.

"It's payback time, Ted," the weathered voice snarled. "Gonna throw you on the train to hell."

Struggling to move, Ted screamed, causing a few heads to turn in his direction. The witnesses looked just in time to see the old man press the tip of his burning cigar into Ted's neck. As the sizzling smell of burnt flesh attracted the senses of those nearby, the old man flew off Ted's body, allowing his victim to rise.

Enraged, Ted charged, but was stopped by the old man's powerful right claw that crushed the abuser's neck and lifted him off the ground. A dozen re-enactors watched as Ted's feet kicked frantically, desperately, performing a spontaneous, but fruitless, air dance.

Ten seconds later, when the lifeless Union corpse hit the Meadow Park grass, everyone nearby stepped back, giving the crazed old man plenty of room.

One witness said, "I saw it all. Scared the hell outta me, I tell you. Then, the guy, the old guy, he says, 'Now we're even.' And then he, like, just up and disappears. It was, like, he was there. Then, like, he was gone. In thin air, at 3 in the afternoon. It was, like, weird, man. Freaked me out, for sure."

Elkton police officers recorded a dozen similar accounts surrounding the unusual, unexplained incident that remains in the department's Unsolved Crimes File.

But Sandy knew the answer to the mystery as soon as the first witness described the stranger—who had thin blue and black streaks running across his forehead and down the side of his face.

Slammin' and Bammin'

"This crap's never gonna go back in the house. You wanna take a piece, go 'head. Be my guest. Nothin' but a royal pain in the you-know-where. But if ya want any, ya better do it tonight, 'cause Ricky, my bother-in-law, is gonna haul it all away for good this weekend. Then, I'll never see the damn stuff again."

That was my introduction to Josh, a 62-year-old retired mechanic who lives in a modest split level house outside Milton, Delaware. His wife, Dolly, reads our ghost books and called me, thinking I would be interested in their story.

She was right.

After a few minutes of conversation on the phone, I made an appointment and visited them two nights later, arriving about 7 o'clock in the evening.

We started out with a friendly hello at the back door, stopped for a brief chat at the kitchen table, progressed to a quick tour of their partially destroyed recreation room and ended up examining thick, weathered beams tossed in a heap on the side of Josh's garage.

But, let's go back to the beginning of the story.

Six months earlier, Josh had bought a truckload of old lumber at a weekend antique sale at an old farmhouse on Maryland's Eastern Shore.

"The dealer didn't get no decent bids," Josh said, "and I was lookin' to get me some beams to accent my rec room ceiling and walls. Them thick, dark wood pieces looked perfect for what I wanted. I didn't think I was gonna be able to afford 'em. But this one slick lookin' guy I was biddin' against, he dropped out, and I got the whole damn cartload for a hundred bucks. Hell, that was a bargain."

With the help of his brother-in-law and two sons, Josh installed the oak beams across the top of his recreation room ceiling and placed several others going up and down the walls at intervals around the room. They were old, heavy and difficult to cut, destroying more than a half-dozen electric saw blades. But Josh said he thought it was well worth the effort.

"I stained them up real good, filled in the cracks with some wood filler. But, mostly, they was in real good shape. Only problem was the cuttin', and then havin' to get enough muscle to hold 'em up to nail and screw 'em in place."

After a few weekends trading beer and sandwiches for cheap labor, the beams were up, accenting the room's white ceiling and red brick walls. A few shorter pieces of the antique lumber served as shelving, holding up Josh's beer can collection and his treasured antique German steins.

"It was a nice job," Dolly said, smiling at Josh. "All the neighbors came over to look and said Josh did good work. We were very happy, and we figured those beams were so sturdy they would be there even if the house caved in."

But they figured wrong.

Leaning forward and looking directly into my eyes, Josh said, rather softly, "All the mess started a little after noon, the very first day after we finished the job. Me and Mother, here, we was both just relaxin' on the front porch and then we both jumped up from our rockers like a bomb up and went off."

I looked from Josh to Dolly.

"That's right," his wife agreed. "It sounded like the ceiling was caving in or like something fell right through the roof. I was scared to death. But Josh, he jumped up, grabbed his pistol from the kitchen and went all around the house to see what happened."

"I checked out the livin' room door," Josh said, "went in the laundry, upstairs, cellar. Nothin', I tell ya. Then, I go into the rec room and I see all my cans is layin' on the rug. Some of them is dented, like they was walked on by somethin'. I looked 'round and everything was locked up tighter than a pig's behind. I couldn't understand it. If it was a earthquake, they woulda just falled off the shelf and hit the floor, but this was like somebody come an' crushed 'em down on purpose. I was really ticked off, for sure."

After cleaning up the room, Josh and Dolly tried to figure out a logical explanation, but there was none.

The next day, the same thing happened—at about the same time, little after noon time.

"Hell," Josh said, shaking his head, "ya coulda set your clock by it. Every damn day, for two full weeks, 'BAM! SLAM!' right after noon, it was."

"As you can imagine," Dolly added, "we couldn't do anything. We just waited around to hear the crashing. For the first three days, we were in different rooms. But after that, we sat in the kitchen, drinking coffee, waiting. Then, right as rain, it would come. The noise, I mean. And we'd get up and rush into the rec room and there would be nothing there. Nothing at all."

After the second day, Josh took down his beer cans and packed away his imported mugs.

"Whatever it was gotmore cans on Day Number Two," he said, snarling. "But I wasn't no idiot. I mean, it don't take a sack of bricks to fall on me to tell me somethin' ain't quite right here. Ya know?"

I nodded and waited for more.

"Anyway," he said, waving his hand across the front of his face and then pointing toward his ripped up recreation room, "I guess ya wanna know why the damn room is torn to hell, right?"

"Sure," I said, encouraging him to continue.

"Look," he said, hesitating, "I know ya ain't gonna believe this, but . . . . Hell! This sounds crazy." Then he turned to Dolly. "Ya gonna tell 'em?"

She smiled and picked up the conversation. "Josh doesn't believe in the supernatural or unearthly, like we do," she said, smiling at me, as her husband shook his head and rolled his eyes. "So, I think I better tell the rest."

Dolly said the crashing sounds continued for the next full week. They set up a tape recorder and captured the noise on a small cassette machine. Placing the black box on the table, she pushed the "play" button and within seconds the "BAM! SLAM" sounds filled the dead space above the kitchen table.

"That's it!" shouted Josh. "That's it, right there, for damn sure! I heard that same crashin' for two full weeks. Even had people come over and sit here and listen for it with us. And it crashed every damn time, like clockwork, right after lunchtime, between 10 and 15 after the hour—as God is my judge."

A neighbor knew a psychic who had lived in San Francisco and had taken courses in meditation and herbal medicine. At Dolly's invitation, the woman came over and tried to help.

"She was a nice lady," Dolly said, "but she left rather quickly after only spending about five minutes in the room. She said the walls were closing in on her and she felt a . . . . Wait, I wrote it down." Looking at a scrap of paper, Dolly said the psychic called it a "negative vibratory field that seriously affected her sensitive extra-dimensional communicative channels."

Slamming his hand on the table, Josh looked at me and asked, "Do you know what the hell that bull crap means?"

I shook my head and said it sounded like somebody using a bunch of big words that don't really say anything.

"Thank God!" Josh shouted, slapping me on the shoulder. "That's just about what I said, 'cept not as nice. Sounds like all that dope she was smokin' and snortin' was finally catchin' up to her. Hell, she come in wearin' some kinda jazzy robes that looked like a flowin' rainbow sheet. Then she starts sprinklin' some spices and magic potion dust . . . ."

"Herbs!" interjected Dolly. "She said they were blessed herbs to chase off the evil spirits."

"Well, it looked like plain old coal ash to me, Doll. And guess who got run'd off. Your friend Sally the Swami," Josh said, turning to me and winking. "That's what I called her, Sally the Swami. Leftover hippie type, if ya ask me."

Dolly said she tried to recontact the psychic soon after that evening visit, but the woman took her time returning the phone calls. When she did, she told Dolly that she did not have an answer to the loud sounds, but they were coming from the recreation room.

"Damn right!" Josh shouted. "Now ain't that a fantabulous freakin' surprise," he added in a mocking tone. "What a freakin', pot smokin' psychotic genius!"

"She did the best she could," Dolly said, trying to defend the woman, then added, "and she didn't charge us anything."

"Good thing!" Josh snapped, shaking his head again and suddenly getting up to get a cold beer from the fridge. Seeing that the conversation was going off in several directions, I started asking a few questions, to pull the focus back to the sounds in the recreation room.

Dolly said that after two full weeks of disruptive days and restless nights, their tolerance had reached its outside limit. Following discussions about the situation with several friends, they all decided that the antique lumber must be the source of their problem. After all, one neighbor said, the noises started immediately after the decorative beams were installed. Before that, there were no strange noises in the home.

Josh's wife mentioned that she had read our book *Possessed Possessions* and that it gave her the idea that the beams might be haunted.

"I tried to talk to the beams, like that lady you wrote about did to her haunted piano down in South Carolina," she said, "but that did no good. They just ignored me. Then, a friend had a son home visiting from college. She told him about the disturbances and he came over with her one afternoon. As his mother and I were talking in the kitchen, he was wandering around the recreation room, rubbing his hands against the beams. First he looked at the ones that were up against the walls. Then he asked if he could bring in a ladder and look more closely at the ones that Josh had installed in the ceiling, and I said, 'Sure.' "

While Dolly and her friend continued their visit, the young man, named Ned, ran his fingers across one of the top beams and seemed to notice a pattern. Over the next half hour, he recorded letters and numbers that had been carved into portions of the beams.

Ned, who was a senior history major at the University in Maryland, asked if he could come back and take a few photographs of the old lumber.

Dolly agreed and Ned returned later that same day.

"We'd already decided to pull the crap down by then," Josh said. "So it didn't matter none, at first, what the college boy was gonna say. When he called a few days later, I had half the beams already outside. He said he wanted to come on over and bring along some graduation student to . . . ."

"*Graduate* student," Dolly corrected.

"Graduate, graduation, what the hell's the difference? Same thing, rich kids with their damn noses in books and all lookin' in them computer screens, gettin' radiated instead of gettin' cancer from too much suntan." Josh laughed at his joke and seemed to enjoy how easily it embarrassed and irritated Dolly.

"Anyway, they come in here and look at the few beams that's left up. Then they go on out back, and are crawlin' and sniffin' like two giant piss ants all over them beams out there in the pile. I keep workin', but then I hear 'em shoutin' and screamin' and pointin' to somethin' in a fat book the one grad-u-*ate* is holdin'."

"They came running up to the back door and asked us both to come outside," Dolly said. "They were very excited, and I was, too, even though I didn't know why. But it seemed that they may have discovered the answer to our problem."

I waited to hear the solution. It was Josh who jumped in and provided the answer.

"The long an' the short of it is this. They show me the name in a book of some fella from Maryland, from up in the Appalachian hills, who made his livin' in the 1800s, goin' from town to town on the Shore buildin' gallows."

"Gallows?" I repeated.

"Yeah! Right! That's 'xactly what I said to 'em, too. It didn't register with me right away neither. These two college boys is tellin' me that I got me lumber from a gallows, a hanging machine, and I put it inside my house for decoration. So I'm thinkin', that's like usin' one a them lethal injection stretchers for a bed. So I run back in and I ripped the rest of this stuff out that night. And that was the last we heard of them noises."

Dolly added an important part to the puzzle. She said the traveling carpenter would carve his initials and date in a certain spot on the beams. That's how Ned and his fellow student were able to identify the gallows. There also were spots in the beams that indicated pieces of hardware and pegs had been present to join the beams together.

"I called the damn auctioneer," said Josh. "Told him I wanted a refund, and he said, 'All sales are final.' Nothin' I could do, and I can't 'xactly go 'round tellin' people I'm hacked off 'cause I bought me a gallows and had a ghost in my house. I'd look like a fool, ya know?"

Walking into the recreation room, Josh pointed to the ripped up ceiling and walls and said, "Now I gotta redo this whole damn room. New drywall, clean up all the brick. Gonna be a hellava job.

But at least the slammin' and bammin's stopped."

Slammin' and bammin'?

"Yeah," Josh said, shaking his head. "Them boys said the noise we heard every day, 'bout just after noontime, was the sounda that gallows trap door openin' and droppin' them bodies down through. See, in the old days, they hanged the poor bastards durin' the daylight, so the town could have a big fair and craft show for all the folks that would come out and take a gander. Was sorta like a church carnival, but the only one who took a ride was the poor bastard they hanged. Did the Eastern Shore air dance."

As Dolly offered a final eye roll, Josh laughed, enjoying his clever commentary. "Now," he added, "this here's one story for your book ya ain't heard before, I bet."

About the Author

Ed Okonowicz, a Delaware native and freelance writer, is an editor and writer at the University of Delaware, where he earned a bachelor's degree in music education and a master's degree in communication.

Also a professional storyteller, Ed is a member of the National Storytelling Association. He presents programs at country inns, retirement homes, schools, libraries, private gatherings, public events, Elderhostels and theaters in the Mid-Atlantic region.

He specializes in local legends and folklore of the Delaware and Chesapeake Bays, as well as topics related to the Eastern Shore of Maryland. He also writes and tells city stories, many based on his youth growing up in his family's beer garden–Adolph's Cafe–in the Browntown section of Wilmington, Delaware.

Ed presents storytelling courses and writing workshops based on his book *How to Conduct an Interview and Write an Original Story*. With his wife, Kathleen, they present a popular workshop entitled, "Self Publishing: All You Need to Know about Getting—or Not Getting—into the Business."

About the Artist

Kathleen Burgoon Okonowicz, a watercolor artist and illustrator, is originally from Greenbelt, Maryland. She studied art in high school and college, and began focusing on realism and detail more recently under Geraldine McKeown. She enjoys taking things of the past and preserving them in her paintings.

Her first full-color, limited-edition print, *Special Places*, features the stately stairway that was the "special place" of the characters in Ed's love story, *Stairway over the Brandywine*.

A graduate of Salisbury State University, Kathleen earned her master's degree in professional writing from Towson State University. She is currently Publications Marketing Manager at the International Reading Association in Newark, Delaware, and a member of the Baltimore Watercolor Society.

For information on storytelling, call Ed. For self-publishing or graphic design assistance, call Kathleen. Telephone: 410 398-5013.

True Ghost Stories from Master Storyteller
Ed Okonowicz

Chills await you in each volume.

Wander through the rooms, hallways and dark corners of this eerie series.

Creep deeper and deeper into terror, until you run Down *the* Stairs *and* Out *the* Door in the last volume of our 13-book series of ghostly tales of the Mid-Atlantic region.

Storytelling World
Honor Award

Delaware Press Association
First Place Award
1997

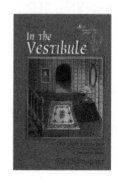

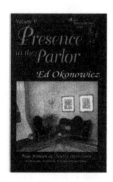

Spirits Between the Bays Series

Volume by volume our haunted house grows. Enter at your own risk!

"If this collection doesn't give you a chill, check your pulse, you might be dead."
–Leslie R. McNair
The Review, University of Delaware

"This expert storyteller can even make a vanishing hitchhiker story fresh and startling."
–Chris Woodyard
owner of Invisible Ink Ghost Catalog
and author of *Haunted Ohio* series

Delaware Press Association
First Place Award
1998

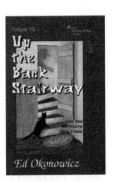

Coming next:
Phantom
in the
Bedchamber

99

The Original

"If you're looking for an unusual gift for a collector of antiques, or enjoy haunting tales, this one's for you."
—Collector Editions

"This book is certainly entertaining, and it's even a bit disturbing."
—Antique Week

". . . an intriguing read."
—Maine Antique Digest

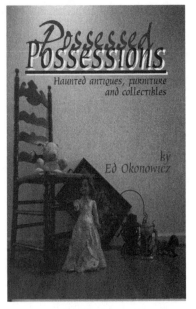

A BUMP. A THUD. MYSTERIOUS MOVEMENT. Unexplained happenings. Caused by What? Venture through this collection of short stories and discover the answer. Experience 20 eerie, true tales about items from across the country that, apparently, have taken on an independent spirt of their own—for they refuse to give up the ghost.

From Maine to Florida, from Pennsylvania to Wisconsin . . haunted heirlooms exist among us . . . everywhere.

Read about them in *Possessed Possessions*, the book some antique dealers *definitely* do not want you to buy.

$9.95

112 pages
5 1/2" x 8 1/2"
softcover
ISBN 0-9643244-5-8

ℓow the Sequel

Across the entire country,
possessed possessions
continue to appear.

Read about 40 more amazing
true tales of bizarre, unusual
and unexplained incidents—all
caused by haunted objects like:
demented dolls
spirited sculptures
pesky piano
killer crib
and much, much more

112 pages
5 1/2" x 8 1/2"
softcover
ISBN 0-890690-02-3

$9.95

WARNING

There could be more than just dust hovering around some of
the items in your home.

The DelMarVa Murder Mystery series

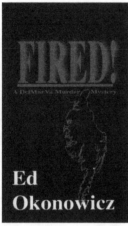

1998

320 pages
4 1/4" x 6 3/4"
softcover
ISBN 1-890690-01-5

$9.95

1999

320 pages
4 1/4" x 6 3/4"
softcover
ISBN 1-890690-03-1

$9.95

Early in the 21st century, DelMarVa, the newest state in the union, which includes Delaware and the Eastern Shore of Maryland and Virginia, is plagued by a ruthless serial killer. In FIRED! meet Gov. Henry McDevitt, Police Commissioner Michael Pentak and State Psychologist Stephanie Litera as they track down the peninsula's worst killer since 19th century murderess Patty Cannon.

In *Halloween House*, the series continues as Gov. McDevitt, Commissioner Pentak and other DelMarVa crime fighters go up against Craig Dire, a demented businessman who turns his annual Halloween show into a real-life chamber of horrors.

The DelMarVa Murder Mystery series continues in the Spring of 2000 with **HOSTAGE,** set at Fort Delaware on Pea Patch Island.

WELCOME

to the

State of

DelMarVa

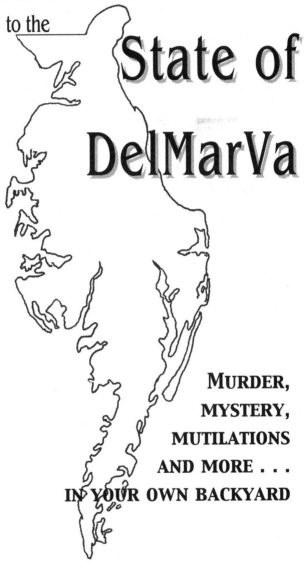

**MURDER,
MYSTERY,
MUTILATIONS
AND MORE . . .
IN YOUR OWN BACKYARD**

Disappearing Delmarva

Portraits of the Peninsula People

Photography and stories by Ed Okonowicz

Disappearing Delmarva introduces you to more than 70 people on the peninsula whose professions are endangered. Their work, words and wisdom are captured in the 208 pages of this hardbound volume, which features more than 60 photographs.

Along the back roads and back creeks of Delaware, Maryland, and Virginia—in such hamlets as Felton and Blackbird in Delaware, Taylors Island and North East in Maryland, and Chincoteague and Sanford in Virginia—these colorful residents still work at the trades that have been passed down to them by grandparents and elders.

208 pages
8 1/2" x 11"
Hardcover
ISBN 1-890690-00-7

$38.00

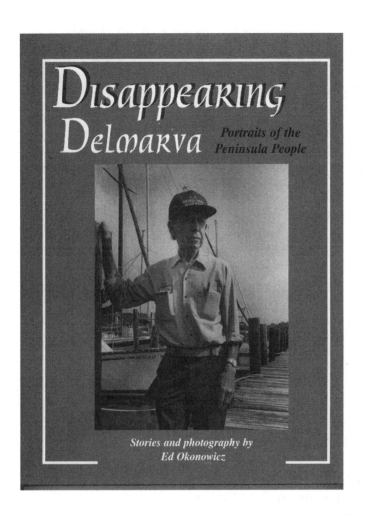

Stories and photography by
Ed Okonowicz

Winner of 2 First-Place Awards:

Best general book
Best Photojournalism entry

National Federation of Press Women Inc.
1998 Communication Contest

To complete your collection. . .
or to be a part of the next book, use the form below:

To submit your personal experience for consideration, to purchase additional books or to be placed on our mailing list, please complete the form below.

Name _____

Address_____

City_____State_____Zip Code_____

Phone Numbers _(_____)_____(_____)_____
       Day   Evening

_____I would like to be placed on the mailing list to receive the free Spirits Speaks newsletter and information on future volumes.

_____I have an experience I would like to share. Please call me.
(Each person who sends in a submission will be contacted. If your story is used, you will receive a free copy of the volume in which your experience appears.)

I would like to order the following books:

Quantity	Title	Price	Total
_____	Pulling Back the Curtain, Vol I	$ 8.95	_____
_____	Opening the Door, Vol II	$ 8.95	_____
_____	Welcome Inn, Vol III	$ 8.95	_____
_____	In the Vestibule, Vol IV	$ 9.95	_____
_____	Presence in the Parlor, Vol V	$ 9.95	_____
_____	Crying in the Kitchen, Vol VI	$ 9.95	_____
_____	Up the Back Stairway, Vol VII	$ 9.95	_____
_____	**Horror in the Hallway, Vol VIII**	**$ 9.95**	_____
_____	Possessed Possessions	$ 9.95	_____
_____	Possessed Possessions 2	$ 9.95	_____
_____	Fired! A DelMarVa Murder Mystery(DMM)	$ 9.95	_____
_____	Halloween House DMM#2	$ 9.95	_____
_____	Disappearing Delmarva	$38.00	_____
_____	Stairway over the Brandywine, A Love Story	$ 5.00	_____

*Md residents add 5% sales tax.
Please include $1.50 postage for the first book, and 50 cents for each additional book.
Make checks payable to:
Myst and Lace Publishers

Subtotal_____
Tax*_____
Shipping_____
Total_____

All books are signed by the author. If you would like the book(s) personalized, please specify to whom.

Mail to: Ed Okonowicz
1386 Fair Hill Lane
Elkton, Maryland 21921